THE RETURN
OF CAULFIELD
BLAKE

THE RETURN
OF CAULFIELD
BLAKE

G. CLIFTON WISLER

M. EVANS
Lanham • Boulder • New York • Toronto • Plymouth, UK

Published by M. Evans
An imprint of Rowman & Littlefield
4501 Forbes Boulevard, Suite 200, Lanham, Maryland 20706
www.rowman.com

10 Thornbury Road, Plymouth PL6 7PP, United Kingdom

Distributed by National Book Network

British Library Cataloguing in Publication Information Available

Library of Congress Cataloging-in-Publication Data

The hardback edition of this book was previously cataloged by the Library of
Congress as follows:

Wisler, G. Clifton
   The return of Caulfield Blake / G. Clifton Wisler.
      p. cm. — (An Evans novel of the West)
   I. Title. II. Series.
   PS3573.I877R4   1987
   813'.54—dc19

                                87-21151

ISBN: 978-1-59077-267-6 (pbk. : alk. paper)
ISBN: 978-1-59077-268-3 (electronic)

∞™ The paper used in this publication meets the minimum requirements of
American National Standard for Information Sciences—Permanence of
Paper for Printed Library Materials, ANSI/NISO Z39.48-1992.

Printed in the United States of America

Chapter One

The Bar Double B spread itself out over a thousand acres of prickly pear and buffalo grass amid the rolling sandstone hills of West Texas. Carpenter Creek cut a broad flood plain through its center, giving birth to stands of live oaks and cottonwoods. Several small springs flowed from the boulder-strewn hillsides, showering the landscape with wildflowers from March to September. It was a good place, near perfect for raising cattle and horses, for building families and futures.

Five or six miles to the north the Colorado River churned its way relentlessly toward the Gulf of Mexico three hundred miles downstream. In summer the river receded, forming great bogs of quicksand that could suck whole wagons under the surface, erasing them forever. In times of heavy rains the river would surge over its banks, sweeping away anything and everything in its path.

No, it was not a tame land. There were always the challenges of drought and flood, heat and cold, birth and death. It produced a hardy people, men and women who survived the worst that nature could throw at them, who thrived where others faltered, and who found it possible to nurture in their children the courage, the strength, and the endurance that allowed them to prosper when it came their time to rule the range.

The original Blake ranch house had been built of stone, a precaution against the Indian raids that had plagued the early settlers of the Texas frontier. In the early 1860s a two-story wooden section had been added to provide rooms for children and a small sitting room. After the war against the North, a further expansion had been made on the west end, a long elbowlike expanse featuring an indoor kitchen, a fancy parlor furnished with a Nashville piano, and a wide veranda for sitting in the cool evening breezes of spring and autumn.

Old Calvin Blake had located the house on a small hill amid a grove of tall white oaks. Several of those trees had yielded the lumber for subsequent additions. A spring formed a small pond behind the house. That pond was the perfect source of drinking water and an ideal spot for a refreshing summer swim. Carpenter Creek lay at the foot of the hill, offering a shield against marauding Indians and water for the vegetables and fruit trees that had been planted along its banks.

Normally in summer the creek lost its power, slowed so that a boy of fourteen might easily cross on foot where he would have been drowned in April. But never had the water fallen so low in early June as it had of late. Hannah had been worried for better than a week about the creek. Only last week there'd been the unmistakable roar of thunder from the southeast, from the granite hills where the creek first emerged from the earth and began its winding, twisting journey to the Colorado. Even so, the creek had continued to evaporate under the relentless Texas sun, shrinking until there was little more than a trickle of water remaining. In some places the creekbed was dry, and the stream had become a series of unconnected puddles.

As she stared at the muddy stream, the creek that was the lifeblood of the ranch and its people, Hannah heard the sound of hooves coming from the dusty road that led from the far side of

Carpenter Creek into the huddle of wooden buildings that constituted the town of Simpson. In another time she would have rushed to the house, taken down the shotgun from its resting place atop the fireplace, and sent one of the children for Marsh. But now she only shielded her eyes from the afternoon sun and tried to make out the face of the rider.

For a moment there was a stir inside her. The man rode a tall brown horse, a stallion by the wild nature of its movements. The rider wore the long gray coat of a Confederate cavalryman, a coat she'd grown familiar with since '62. But as the horseman approached, she felt a sigh wriggle its way through her being. It was not, could not be the one she'd imagined. No, he was far away.

Dixon Stewart slowed his horse to a canter and splashed his way through the shallow remnant of the creek. He drew the stallion to a halt, then waited for Hannah to speak.

"Good afternoon, Dix," she said, managing a smile. "You appear to be in a Yankee hurry today."

"It's old man Simpson," Dixon said, frowning. "He's gone and built a dam across the creek. It's makin' a lake out of Siler's Hollow. In another month, we'll be bone dry."

"I don't see how that's possible," she said. "Dix, you can't build a dam out of this fool sand we've got here. Marsh tried digging an irrigation channel off the Colorado. It just won't work."

"Marsh didn't have fifty men workin' on it. He didn't move rocks, whole wagons full of 'em."

"It doesn't make sense. The Simpson ranch doesn't use the sections that border our ranches. The range along Carpenter Creek's no good to him. A hundred gullies must lie in the way. He'd lose more cows the first week than he could get through a summer's grazing."

"Not if he joined our land to his."

"Now how's he going to do that?"

"By dryin' us out."

"But why? He's got more acreage than he could ride in a month of Sundays."

"Maybe he's grown tired of neighbors."

"After all these years?"

"Maybe it's not all these years he's thinkin' on, Hannah. Maybe it's only the last seven."

"He wouldn't bear a grudge that long."

"He's near seventy, and he's had little more to think about. I've seen those eyes of his. I've read death before."

"So what do we do? We've got a right to the water."

"Right? Hannah, when you and I and Caulie . . ."

She frowned, and Dixon coughed away the rest of the sentence.

"Well?" she asked.

"Before the war, when we were both a whole lot younger, old Judge Harper sat the bench. We could count on justice. But since that carpetbagger Derry got himself shot, all we've had on the bench is one thief after another sent up from Austin. Now there's no one at all."

"You can ride to the capital yourself. Marsh and I'll look after Rita and the children."

"And what will I plead? Simpson pays more taxes than the balance of the county combined. You think the governor'll even see me, much less listen?"

"We have to do something."

"We should have," Dixon said, sighing. "A long time ago. We should have been a little stronger seven years back when it would've been easy. All Simpson had on his side then was public feeling. People were swayed by sentiment. We might have changed all that. Now it seems like the old man's got a hundred hands on his place, cash in the bank, and a hunger for more."

"You're upset."

"A bit. Haven't I been preachin' about everybody stickin' together? Didn't I tell you when the Mexicans got run off Simpson wouldn't stop there? And what about the Carlsons and the Brocks?"

"That's history, Dix. What do we do now?"

"I don't know," he said, throwing his arms up in despair. "I guess find a market for my horses and cattle. Hope maybe that dam springs itself a leak and the flood won't take my house."

"There has to be something more."

"Like what? Maybe you think Marsh and I ought to ride out and ask Simpson if he'd please let a little water down the creekbed. Or maybe we ought to hire somebody to shoot the old man. But then we'd have to deal with his grandson Matt, and I'd rather wrestle a mountain cat."

"What are you getting at, Dix? I know you too well. You aren't going to give up without a fight."

"I can't do it alone, Hannah. Marsh won't be much help. We need someone with experience, someone who won't buckle under."

"Or didn't?" she asked, trembling as the vision of a face appeared in her mind, a tall man with broad shoulders and bright blue eyes that always sparkled when she was around.

"He'd come if you wrote him," Dixon said, his eyes growing solemn. "If you said you needed him."

"It's been too long," she said, looking at her feet.

"Think about the boys. Wouldn't hurt to see their father."

"Marsh is their father."

"I'll admit Marsh's done right by 'em, but it's not the same as bein' their blood father. Hannah, I know it's hard. It hurts your pride. But do it for us all, for Marty Cabot and me and, yes, even for Marsh."

"Marsh'd die before he'd ask for help from . . ."

"I know that. Don't you think it pains me to bring up the subject to you? But, Hannah, I don't see we've got any choice."

"It's what Simpson expects. It's why . . ."

"Maybe."

"I won't ask him to come, not to ride down here knowing that old man's sworn to see him dead."

"Well, we've talked about us. We've talked about Simpson. What about Caulie?"

"Go on."

"What will he feel when he learns there's been trouble and you didn't send word? You know where he's at?"

"He writes at Christmas. For the boys."

"Joe Stovall saw him in Abilene. Was raisin' horses."

"He's good at that."

"Hannah, he's good at more'n that. He's the best man I ever knew at siftin' through a problem and findin' its root. And I never saw another man do so much with so little."

"I don't know," she said, shaking her head. "What right have I got to ask him to come back? When he needed me, I let him go." She could feel her hands trembling. "Maybe he wouldn't come anyway. He's started a whole new life."

"You know better. He never forgets you. All through the war, even when we were cold and hungry and almost out of hope, he never stopped talkin' about you."

"That was a long time ago."

"Was it?"

She closed her eyes and remembered that last time he'd stood beside her on the veranda, their hands intertwined. She'd prayed he wouldn't go.

"You don't have to do it," she'd said. "No one will give you a medal or even thank you. The Yankees won't. They only use men like you to do the dirty work."

"It's a duty."

"The whole town will turn against us. The boys won't be welcome at school. I won't be able to hold my head up in church."

"I have to, Hannah. I swore an oath."

"Not to be a hangman. Not to kill Henry Simpson's son."

"The law can't just be for Jody Morgan or Curtis French. It's got to be for everyone."

"You care more for that badge, that fool piece of tin, than you do for us, for Carter and Zach and me."

"It's not the badge," he'd said, taking it off his coat. "I told you. I'll resign tomorrow. But I can't back down from an obligation."

"It's only pride. Stubborn pride. Well, you go on and do your duty, Caulie. And afterward you find yourself another place to come home to because you won't be welcome here."

"You don't mean that," he'd said, leaning against the wooden bench. "Don't ask me to make that kind of a choice."

"I don't have to," Hannah had told him. "You already did."

Marty'd sent word, how Caulie had lain in the street, his clothes torn and tattered, his face swollen with bruises. And she'd . . .

"Hannah, are you all right?" Dix asked, grabbing her as her legs gave way. "Hannah?"

"How can I write him?" she asked, her eyes ablaze with emotion. "How can I ask him to come back now when I wouldn't take him in then?"

But Dix didn't answer. They both knew she would write. And deep down inside herself she knew he'd come, would always come. That was the worst part of all.

Chapter Two

The broad plain south of the Clear Fork of the Brazos River was once dotted with buffalo. The great woollies were mostly gone now, slaughtered by hide hunters in the preceding decade. Cattle were arriving to take their place, rugged longhorn steers that had given birth to a new Texas economy following the devastation of war and reconstruction. The railroad was creeping ever westward, bringing with it people and civilization. Eighteen-eighty was witnessing an end to the unbridled freedoms of the frontier as they gave way to farms and ranches, towns and churches.

Not far from the cavalry post at Fort Griffin lay the ramshackle collection of wooden huts and gambling houses known as The Flat. In its earlier days it had seen wild brawls and gunfights in its dusty streets. Thousands of dollars changed hands at the end of the buffalo-hunting season.

The town had sheltered more than its share of notorious characters, everyone from Wyatt Earp and Bat Masterson to Big Nose Kate Elder and Lottie Deno, the queen of the poker table. They'd moved on now, as had all but a shadow of the cavalry.

What remained of the place provided comfort and diversion to the soldiers and supplies to the ranches that had begun appearing in Shackelford County.

Just across the river from The Flat lay a picket cabin of earth and logs. A horse corral stood nearby, shaded by the cottonwoods that spread out from the river. On any given day the corral might contain a dozen mustang ponies, rounded up from the plain. An occasional army mount might be there as well, retrieved from a renegade Comanche or army deserter and awaiting redemption at the standard rate promised by the post commander.

That particular morning two young men were busy with the ponies. The third, an older man, sat on a boulder preparing to read a letter. Those who knew Caulfield Blake wouldn't have been concerned by his somber appearance, the cold eyes and the stiff posture. He was nearing forty, a long life for a man who'd ridden four years with Forrest, endured seven long cattle drives north to Kansas, and spent the last four years chasing mustangs on the plains.

But there *was* something different about him. His hands trembled slightly as he tore open the simple white envelope and began reading.

"My dear Caulie," the words said. "All has not been well with us of late."

The trembling grew worse as the words swept through his mind. He could hear her speaking, remember her face, the softness of her touch.

"Colonel Simpson has taken it in his head to build a dam across Carpenter Creek. Dix Stewart suggested you might help us. I know it will not be easy for you to return, but your family and friends are in need of your help. Please come."

The letter was signed simply "Hannah." There was no "affectionately yours" as in those longer, passionate notes written during the war.

"Why should I?" he asked, staring at the horses.

He reread the words. Dix suggested, did he? Things couldn't

be well if Dix needed help. No one, excepting perhaps himself, found it more difficult to ask help than Dix Stewart.

"Simpson!" The word left a sour taste in his mouth even now. Colonel Simpson? What had the old man ever commanded that gave him the right to that title? It was a mockery of everything Blake had fought for, a corruption of the concept of honor itself. Yes, honor. For Caulfield Blake, honor had always exacted a high price. He'd ached and bled across a hundred fields during the war, driven on when others scurried away because duty had always demanded sacrifice from the Blakes. Only after Bedford Forrest himself declared the cause lost had Blake's Texans turned their horses homeward. Then, back home among the familiar rocks and hills above Carpenter Creek, duty had called again.

It was Simpson himself that had offered the five-pointed star to Caulfield Blake.

"Your father settled this county when there were more Comanches hereabouts than rattlesnakes," the old man had said. "People know the name Blake, and your wartime service hasn't hurt you any. These Yanks have bought your horses. They think they can trust you to uphold justice."

Those words had drawn Blake into Simpson's web, attracted him like a juicy carrot entices a cantankerous mustang. Blake hadn't noticed the brooding eyes that lurked behind Simpson's easy smile and disarming manner.

"Don't do it," Hannah had warned. "No Simpson's ever done a Blake or a Siler a favor without measuring its price on a loaded scale. He'll blame you for every hardship, Caulie, and he'll heap all the unpleasant tasks on your doorstep."

But the other choice had been to accept a dozen bluecoat soldiers permanently stationed at the courthouse. Caulfield Blake pinned on the badge.

For a time all had gone well. Blake chased a band of renegades off the range and sent a road agent named Maley along to the State Police in Austin. He organized the farms and ranches against Comanche raiders, and the Indians found the price of stealing beeves and horses too high. Then, when it seemed that perhaps the war could be put behind them all, an Indiana judge named Franklin Derry arrived in Simpson and took over the courthouse.

No sooner had the dust from Derry's coach settled than the judge was announcing new taxes.

"You people have had it far too easy," Derry declared. "The values placed on your land are too low by half. We'll tend to that."

Each ranch and farm felt the bite of Derry's tax bills, but the Simpson place, being largest, was hurt worst of all. And when the "colonel" couldn't bribe or threaten his way out of payment, open war erupted.

"It's up to you to collect these monies," Judge Derry had told Blake.

"I won't," Blake had responded. "They're your taxes. You collect 'em."

Derry had grinned and walked straight to the telegraph office. In three days a company of soldiers arrived to do the collecting. Those lacking the cash found themselves stripped of every possession. Confiscated livestock filled a corral, and the ground floor of the courthouse was crammed with furniture and assorted articles of clothing and hardware. Only those few fortunate ranchers like Blake and Dix Stewart who'd sold horses and cattle to the bluecoat cavalry had Yankee dollars to pay the heavy taxes. The hardest hit glared with contempt at the tin star on Caulfield Blake's shirt.

"Simpson stirs 'em up," Dix complained. "That old buzzard's gone around tellin' how you rode two of his boys to their graves in the war. As if you weren't out there in front every single time! And him callin' himself colonel now, too! Caulie, trouble's bound to come o' this."

And it had. When Simpson's friends in Austin hadn't been able to help him evade the taxes or replace Franklin Derry, Simpson sent his youngest son, thirty-year-old Austin, to tend to the matter. An hour short of twilight on a brisk Wednesday in mid-March, Austin Simpson drew a pistol and shot Judge Derry four times.

Even those who hadn't cared much for the carpetbagger judge were stunned. And when Austin paraded through town boasting of the act, the soldiers acted. A young lieutenant arrested Austin and dragged the young man toward the livery. Halfway there a mob of Simpson ranch hands clubbed the officer to death and set Austin loose.

Open warfare broke out. Austin led his father's hands across the valley, threatening neighbors and hunting down any blue-coats that emerged from town. The cavalry reacted by sending a whole company down from Fort Griffin.

"They'll kill my boy," Simpson said when he pleaded with Blake to ride out after Austin. "I lost the others fighting Yankees. They were good soldiers. You led 'em yourself, Blake. Don't let these Yanks kill Austin."

"He'll come to trial if he gives up," Blake promised. "After that, it's up to the court. You know half the town saw him shoot that judge. He's like as not to hang."

"Anything can happen in a courtroom," Simpson had said, grinning. "You just get him back to town."

"I was a fool," Blake mumbled, staring out across the broken prairie. "Henry Simpson never told the straight truth a day in his whole life."

Long, hard years of war had taken their toll, and the years of peace that had followed had too often been torn by Comanche raids and violent ambushes. Too many friends had been buried. Caulfield Blake set off into the hills alone. And though bands of cavalry crisscrossed the hills above the Colorado in search of Austin Simpson, Blake located the young killer almost immediately. On a moonless night the first week of April, Blake slipped past Austin's cohorts, clubbed the outlaw across the head, and sneaked him five miles through friend and foe to the jailhouse in Simpson.

"I brought him in," Blake told Henry Simpson. "Now it's up to the law."

Simpson never replied. Instead he brought in lawyers from New Orleans and made speeches about a higher authority than statehouses and courtrooms.

"No jury in Texas will find my boy guilty," Simpson cried. "He's a patriot like his fallen brothers, a hero to his native land."

The trial went sour early. The Republican governor sent out a smart lawyer from Austin to argue the state's case, and the three New Orleans dandies spent most of their time making grand speeches. The Austin prosecutor just got one witness after another to swear Austin Simpson shot the judge down in the streets. No one knew Derry to carry so much as a pocket pistol.

"Austin Simpson did his county a service by ridding it of a bloodsucking tyrant," one lawyer countered. Another quoted from *Julius Caesar*.

"These folks saw what they saw," the prosecutor reminded the jury. "You can't find Austin Simpson other than guilty of cold-blooded murder."

And so they did. The hangman arrived the following day, and a gnarled old oak just outside of town was chosen as the gallows. A pair of soldiers erected a small stand with a trapdoor. Their hammering sent shivers down Caulfield Blake's back.

"No one'd ever know if you were to take an early supper and leave the keys on your desk," Simpson said the day before the hanging was to take place. "You might find a way for Austin to slip away when you take him out in the morning. Lots of things could happen."

"I've sworn to do my duty," Blake declared. "I will."

"Duty! That's what Austin did."

"He did your biddin', Simpson. He'll hang for that. You valued the feel of gold coins and Yankee bank notes above a man's life. Now the law's callin' for payment."

"You can't hang my boy."

"I'm not. The law will."

"If Austin dies in the morning, I'll see you pay for it. You brought him in. People will remember that. You rode young Henry and Matthew to their graves as well. You've got boys, Blake! How'd you like to see them swinging from an oak limb?"

"You watch your words, Simpson! You'd not care to have this hornet buzzin' around your head. I sting hard."

"I swat the likes of you into the dust every day, Blake. I sent your daddy to an early grave, and there are spades aplenty about. I can bury you easy enough."

"Can you?"

"Watch me."

Even now, after seven long years, Caulfield Blake recalled the fire in Simpson's eyes. The memory of that time remained sharp. It was, after all, etched deeply in his heart.

Blake left the jailhouse early, but a squadron of cavalry guarded the doors. Soldiers patrolled the streets like an occupying army. Bitter townsfolk stared at the shiny brass buttons and recalled sons and husbands who'd fallen at Vicksburg and Chickamauga.

"Pa, don't go back to town," seven-year-old Carter pleaded that night after a silent dinner. "I hear people talk. They say they'll hang others if Austin dies."

"It's my job, my duty," Blake explained. But Carter was eaten by a hundred nightmares, and the words of his father had no effect.

"You never asked to be sheriff," Hannah complained. "I never wanted it. Lord knows I gave you up to duty four long years. That's enough to ask of any woman. Give them back their star. Leave the soldiers to finish it. They will, you know."

"And if the people try to stop it? The soldiers have rifles. Those are my friends in town. Can I stay out here and leave 'em to die?"

"What do you think will happen if you go? Don't you know Colonel Simpson blames you for Austin's capture, the trial, the

14

hanging? Those people you call your friends aren't going to watch that boy hang and forgive it. If they can't avenge themselves on the soldiers, they can easily enough find you. And us."

"Hannah?"

"I've seen mobs, Caulie. I watched some of these peaceful neighbors of ours tear apart a Comanche boy Ben Stovall knocked senseless during the war. You'll be killed, and for what?"

"I have to do it, Hannah."

"Stubborn! You always have been, but this time you're risking everything. Carter and little Zach, too. Get Dix and Marty to go along."

"I won't bring trouble to my friends."

"No? Just to your family?"

"Hannah, that's not what I mean."

"Then hear me, Caulie! If you ride into town tomorrow, don't bother coming back. There'll be no place for you. For too many nights I went to bed expecting to hear in the morning that you had been killed in Tennessee. I won't go back to that, not ever again."

The words tore at him, sliced deep into his heart.

"You can't mean that, Hannah. You . . . I love you. You mean the world to me."

"Then stay."

"You know I can't do that."

"Then go," she'd said, her eyes turning dark and stormy as never before. In saying it, she'd retired to their bedroom and thrown his clothes in a chest which she dragged onto the porch.

They spoke a final time the next morning. The words were little different, though.

"You go and do your duty, Caulie," she'd spoken with stinging fury. "And afterward you find another place to come home to, because you won't be welcome here."

He'd saddled his horse and ridden off with nary a farewell wave.

She'd been right about the town. An angry mob gathered around the oak and watched as Caulfield Blake escorted a sobbing, trembling Austin Simpson to the makeshift gallows. Nearby Henry Simpson huddled with Austin's dainty wife and young son.

"There'll be a price paid for this murder!" the old man cried out. The people murmured their agreement, and a few stones flew toward the gallows. A line of soldiers leveled their rifles, and Blake pleaded for peace.

"We'll settle with you later," someone bellowed. A stone clipped Blake's shoulder. He swallowed the pain and fought to maintain order. A graying cavalry captain motioned to the hooded hangman, and the trap sprung. Austin Simpson fell quickly, and the murderer's neck snapped abruptly.

"Thank God it's over," the captain mumbled.

But it was anything but over. The soldiers loaded Austin Simpson's body in a wagon, then marched back to the courthouse. Blake had already handed the captain his badge and was headed for his horse when a pair of Simpson hands stepped out of the shadows. Another and another arrived afterward. Soon a dozen men collected in a circle, and suddenly fists came from everywhere.

Blake only felt the first few punches. Soon his eyes were swollen closed, and the blows of planks and toes smashing ribs and legs were beyond him. He drifted off long before Henry Simpson arrived with a can of blue paint to pour on the motionless body of Caulfield Blake. He never saw the small boy spit or the ashen-faced widow curse.

For two days Caulfield Blake was as good as dead. He regained consciousness in the half-completed barn of Marty Cabot.

"Thought you dead for certain this time, Cap'n," Marty said with the same broad smile that had been directed at federal cavalry fleeing from Brice's Crossroads a decade earlier. "They did you up fine. Took Dix and me three hours to wash all that blue paint out o' your hide."

"Paint?"

"Colonel Simpson's notion, I suspect. Don't try to move just yet. Half your ribs must be cracked. They broke your nose again. Left leg's a little sour, too."

"Hannah?"

Marty hadn't answered for a time. When he did, the pain from his fractured ribs and aching head ebbed as a new wave of sorrow overwhelmed him.

"She won't come, Cap'n. Says she said all that's to be said. Doesn't mean it, though. I could tell she's hurtin' for you."

But days passed into weeks, and Hannah never came. Bones mended, and spirits revived, but Hannah never relented.

"There's mighty bad blood about," Mary explained. "Cap'n, maybe we ought to take a ride out west, run down some mustangs, sell some to the army and maybe buy some acreage up north, maybe on the Brazos."

"She doesn't want me back."

"She never said it so I'd believe it, Cap'n."

"She doesn't have to," Blake had said sadly. "She told me plain enough. On the Brazos, you say?"

"Plenty of buffalo up there, or so I hear. Mustangs that can chase your heart to Colorado."

It had sounded good, a fresh start. And if he hadn't looked behind when he crossed the Colorado, it wasn't because he hadn't left anyone or anything behind. His heart would always be there, his heart and his blood. Even now he ached with a longing to feel Hannah's gentle hands in his own, to touch the boys, to share his heart with that other part of himself left so long ago back on Carpenter Creek.

"Ben, Frank," Blake said, turning to the two young men at the corral. "I've got to ride down south for a time."

"What?" the first one, a thin-faced eighteen-year-old named Ben Harris, asked. "We've got a dozen horses to deliver to the Kensingtons next week. And four promised to Major Plumb."

"Captain," the second man said, walking to the gate, "how long'll you be gone?"

"A week, maybe more. Could be I won't make it back at all."

Ben started to say something, but the other man, Frank Parker, gestured for silence.

"Captain," Frank said, "we been riding out there three summers now. You knew my daddy. When a man rides with me, his troubles come to be my troubles. I never knew you to get a letter from Simpson in the summer."

Blake frowned. Frank Parker wasn't more than twelve when the Simpson trouble had occurred. The young man would soon turn twenty and was as ready to take up arms as the brother who'd fallen at Johnsonville in '64.

"No, it's your place to stay here," Blake said. "This is a personal thing."

"Kensington won't be any too pleased you left us to fill his contract," Ben complained. "He'll likely want to cut the price."

"You leave that to Frank," Blake said, spitting away the last bit of tobacco juice from his morning plug. "Walt Kensington will deal fairly with you if you take him twelve good mounts. And you will."

"Captain . . ." Frank began.

"You two'll do just fine," Blake told them. "You're both good men with a rope. And if I don't make it back . . ."

The three of them sat stone-faced a second as Blake tried to complete the thought.

"We'll make out," Frank said. "Even if I have a skinny no-account like Ben here for a partner."

Ben started to object, but Blake turned and started toward the house. A few moments later Blake reemerged from the cabin with blanket roll, a knapsack, and two saddlebags. Frank helped saddle a horse, and after another uncomfortable silence, Caulfield Blake mounted a big black stallion and splashed his way across the river, bound for the Colorado and the town he thought he'd left behind forever seven years ago.

Chapter Three

No one walking the streets of Simpson forgot that dusty July afternoon that Caulfield Blake rode into town. He was no ordinary man. His six-foot two-inch frame gave him an appearance larger than life as he sat atop his great black stallion. A week's growth of beard made his face seem dark, menacing. Those piercing blue eyes that had alternately struck enemies with fear and comrades with devotion swept the streets, observing everything, noticing even the smallest detail. Long strands of dark brown hair sprinkled with traces of gray curled under and around a faded brown leather drover's hat.

He wore buckskin trousers and a cotton shirt, a combination which seemed strange to the onlookers. Around his waist was a black Confederate officer's belt, with its accompanying Colt revolver resting on his right hip.

If the town seemed preoccupied with Blake, Blake was no less taken aback by the town.

"It's changed," he mumbled as he nudged the horse toward a brightly painted building with a hand-lettered sign over the door,

STEWART'S. Sitting on a bench beside the door was a small blond boy of ten or so. Blake climbed down from the horse, tied the reins to a post, and approached the boy.

"Dix around?" Blake asked.

"Out to the ranch today," the boy said, shrinking back from Blake's steellike gaze. "Got business with him?"

"Might have. Let's see now. You'd be ten April last, as I recall. Your papa named you Charles, but it's likely come to be Charlie by now."

"You know Papa?"

"About since the first time he threw me off into the creek down in Siler's Hollow."

The conversation was interrupted by the appearance of a girl. She had her brother's fair hair and deep brown eyes, but her face revealed suspicion and suggested caution.

"Can I help you, mister?" she asked.

"And you'd be Katherine," Blake said, moving the boy forward with a weathered right hand as they entered the store together.

"And who might you be?" she challenged. "I got no uncles, and I don't take to liars."

"Or baths, either, as I remember. I'll bet they call you Kate."

The boy nodded, and Blake's eyes brightened. The beginning of a smile appeared on his lips.

"Just who are you?" Kate asked, retreating to where a shotgun rested beside the cash drawer back of the counter.

"Let's see if I can help you figure it out. There was a man here a few years ago. You used to complain about his mustache. Made it tickle when you kissed him."

"Lots of men have whiskers."

"Well, that's true enough. But how many know about that little heart-shaped mark on your . . ."

"Stop right there!" she said, her face growing bright red. "I don't see how you could know about that."

"Oh, I might could if I had to give you a bath. You weren't too agreeable to it, I admit, tossin' soapy water in my eyes, bitin' my fingers."

"You're him," she suddenly blurted out, trembling.

The boy seemed confused, but Kate walked briskly to an old desk beside the window and took out a yellowing photograph. Five soldiers sat together under a Tennessee oak tree. Kate pointed to the tall, dark-haired young man in the center. Blake nodded.

"Uncle Caulie," she said, wrapping both arms around his dusty waist and hugging tightly. "I remember."

Blake pulled the boy over and squeezed his thin shoulder.

"Papa didn't expect you to come to town," Kate said. "You might should leave. Colonel Simpson's at the hotel."

"Good. It's best he know right away."

Kate's forehead wrinkled, but Blake smiled away her concern.

"He'd know sooner or later," Charlie mumbled. "He finds out everything."

"Well, money can buy a lot of information in a town like this one," Blake said bitterly. "Money can buy lots of things."

Yes, he thought, remembering the angry crowd that had torn him off his horse, beaten him with sticks, robbed him of his home, his family. He recalled the faces, those people who'd begged him to take on the duties as sheriff when he had a world of work to do at the ranch. Where had they been when the crisis came? They'd kept to the shadows, then jumped like a pack of wolves at his back.

"I'll see your horse gets some water," Charlie said, touching Blake lightly on the arm before leaving.

"Be careful," Kate warned as Blake turned and started for the street.

"Never been one to walk lightly," he said, taking a deep breath. Then he started for the hotel.

People stepped back into doorways and scrambled for cover when they saw Blake. Few recognized his face, but there was no mistaking the glare in those defiant eyes, the strong, determined walk of the soldier he'd been most of his life. When he marched through the open door of the hotel, the half-dozen people in the lobby grew silent.

"Excuse me, sir," said the desk clerk, "but the hotel's reserved this week. Colonel Simpson's expecting cattle buyers."

"Why don't you tell the *colonel* someone's here to see him?"

"And who might that be?" a young man asked from the sofa.

Blake turned in that direction. The young man wore a tailored suit and one of those short-rimmed hats that had become fashionable in Austin. His legs were long and thin, and no whiskers were as of yet growing on his face. He couldn't have celebrated his eighteenth birthday, but he was wearing a pistol under his coat. The long blond hair, the arrogant brown eyes reminded Blake of all the Simpsons.

"I might be just about anyone," Blake said. "As it happens, my name is Blake."

"Caulfield Blake?" young Simpson asked as a hush swept the room.

"I figured you might recognize the name."

"Oh, dear," a woman near the door said.

"Mr. Blake, I'd appreciate it if you'd go elsewhere," the clerk said.

"I'll get my grandfather," the young man said, nervously watching Blake while backing his way up the stairs.

The hotel lobby emptied as Blake waited for Simpson. When the old man finally appeared, his wrinkled face filled with rage. Simpson needed the grandson's help to negotiate the steps. Finally, the two old enemies stood face to face.

"Blake, I warned you never to come back," the old man shouted. "I'll see you dead this time."

"You've done your warnin', old man," Blake said, never flinching. "I told you somethin', too. I told you to leave my family be. If you need to blame somebody for your boy bein' a murderer, then blame me. Hannah never caused you pain."

"She's a Blake," Simpson said, spitting on the rich carpet of the hotel. "That's enough. And she gave birth to two Blake pups."

"Look, Simpson, eight years ago you came to me and asked me to be sheriff of this town. You asked me to swear to uphold the laws. You didn't say anythin' about lookin' the other way when your boy shot a judge in cold blood right in the middle of Front Street."

"That judge was a carpetbagger, a thief. He was no better'n a snake. You shoot snakes."

"He was a man, no better or worse in the eyes of the law than Henry Simpson or Caulfield Blake. I didn't ask for that badge. You and the others, you put it all on me. Then when the soldiers came and expected justice, you turned away. Afterward your brave bunch of men came after me."

"You hung my son, Matt's father."

The young man glared at Blake. A trace of viciousness appeared in the corner of his eyes.

"I helped execute a killer. He had a fair trial before a jury of his peers. You could have appealed."

"To Yankees? To the same men who killed two of my boys at Selma?"

"I fought in the war, too, remember? I didn't sit behind a desk and call myself colonel when the smoke cleared."

The comment brought a shiver of rage to the old man's face. Blake only smiled.

"You've been warned, Blake," Simpson shouted. "The next time you show your face in this town, someone'll put a bullet through it right in between your eyes!"

"Oh?" Blake asked, chuckling. "You think maybe you can pay someone a few hundred dollars to do that? Or will you face me yourself? Why wait? Why not right now?"

Young Matt started toward Blake, but his grandfather held him back. Then the sheriff walked through the door, a Winchester rifle in his hands. Blake moved aside and let the lawman take over.

"I think it's best you leave," the sheriff said to Blake. "Colonel, maybe you ought to have a little rest. You seem a bit flushed."

Simpson smiled.

"You remember what I said, Blake!" the old man shouted.

23

"Oh, I will," Blake told him. "And you keep in mind that I won't look kindly on you troublin' Hannah and the boys."

Before the old man could say anything more, Blake turned and slipped quietly out of the hotel. He soon spotted his horse at a watering trough in front of the Palace Saloon. He walked cautiously the hundred yards to the horse, accepted the reins from Charlie, and climbed into the saddle.

"Tell Dix to come see me," Blake told the boy. "And tell him to keep a weather eye out for Simpson. The old man's capable of anythin'."

"Yes, sir," Charlie said.

Blake then turned the horse toward the far end of town and began the five-mile ride to the Bar Double B. Home. For the first time since arriving in town he trembled.

Chapter Four

Blake rode along the dusty road almost without thinking. The seven years he'd been away had not erased the memories accumulated in a lifetime of riding those hills. He passed the oak grove where he'd asked Hannah to be his wife. He paused near Siler's Hollow to recall the times he'd chased Dix and Marty Cabot through the high grasses. But the hollow was now flooded by an ocean of water. And Carpenter Creek . . . well, it was little more than a hog wallow.

The ranch appeared to have prospered in his absence. There were fences along the boundaries now, and the peach trees he and Hannah had planted on their wedding day stood tall alongside the creekbed. He saw hundreds of cattle on the range, tough steers ready for market, cows that would provide fresh milk and increase the herd, and three powerful bulls for breeding. But the trees appeared dry, and the animals seemed thirsty.

Another week and the creek would be barren. What then?

The one eternal truth of West Texas life was that without water, a ranch was only so much dust doomed to blow in the wind. All the building, the back-breaking work done by three generations to build the Bar Double B was useless if Carpenter Creek dried up.

"What manner of man waves his hand and brings death to all this?" Blake asked himself as he surveyed his former homestead from the crest of a small rise. Across the creek stood the house. His eyes swept from the vegetable gardens to the corral, from the swing which hung beneath the tall white oak to the distant barn.

He then started across what was left of the creek, carefully avoiding the stretches that seemed likely hosts for quicksand. As he started up the hill toward the house, he drew his horse short and stared at two small boys playing near the chicken coop.

They were far too young to be Carter or Zach. There was a girl, too, a small thing dressed in a bright yellow sun dress. His eyes lingered as they fell on a more familiar figure, a woman whose petite frame and flowing blond hair concealed an inner strength he'd known but once in his entire life.

"Hannah?" he called to her.

She waved, not with the excitement he'd expected, but casually, almost as if performing a scene from a play. As Blake approached, a man stepped out of the house, a large, muscular man with thinning brown hair and a large black mustache.

Blake slowed his horse and sat atop the saddle for a moment, watching her, waiting, trying to think of something to say.

"I, uh, I came," he finally stammered.

"I knew you would," she said sadly.

Blake dismounted, leaving his horse to chew the soft grass on the hillside. He wanted to reach out and hold her, lift her off the ground with a whirl the way he used to.

"You remember Marsh Merritt," Hannah said nervously. "I wrote you . . . about us."

"How are you?" Blake asked, extending a reluctant hand toward the man.

"Don't know what point there was to sending for you, Blake," Marsh said. "This is my place now. I'll tend to Simpson."

Blake glanced around. He hoped to catch a glimpse of his boys, but they were nowhere to be found. The younger boys had Marsh's dark hair, his thick shoulders. But the girl was Hannah reborn.

"There've been a lot of changes since you left," Marsh went on. "We concentrate on cattle now, only raise enough horses for our needs."

"Oh?"

Marsh went on to point out the new barn, the expanded gardens. Blake nodded, but he didn't pay much attention.

"I guess it was a mistake my comin'," Blake said, frowning. "I'll ride on to Dix's place."

"No, wait," Hannah said, taking Blake's hand and holding him there. "Caulie, stay."

"He's got a right to do as he will," Marsh said.

"I know this is hard on you, Marsh," she said, releasing Blake's hand and turning toward her husband. "It's going to be a strain for us all. But I asked him to come, and it's not proper to turn him away now. Besides, we *do* need him."

"I can do anything that needs to be done," Marsh growled, a hint of bitterness in his voice. "There's not room here for the both of us, Hannah."

"It's better I go," Blake said. "I don't mean to come as an intruder."

"Intruder?" Hannah cried. "You grew up on this ranch. You built half the house with your own hands. You owe it to the boys, to yourself to stay. And I wouldn't have sent the letter if we didn't need you. Marsh," she said, turning away from Blake, "will you fetch Carter and Zach? Tell them they have a visitor."

Marsh frowned. Reluctantly he started back to the house.

"You have to understand, Caulie," Hannah said quietly as she led the way to the veranda. "We've been very happy."

"He seems a good man. Why did you send for me? He appears willin' and able to deal with the problem."

"Marsh is good and kind and gentle. He's got a natural way with growing things. But he's never fired a shot in anger, not even at a prowling bobcat. He wouldn't know how to answer Henry Simpson."

"And I would?"

"Yes," she said sadly. "You did once."

"And it cost me everythin' I ever held dear."

"I know," Hannah said, looking away. "Why is it we do and say things we don't mean, Caulie? Why do we let pride and duty get in the way of what's really important?"

"Duty is important, Hannah."

"Not that duty. If only you could have turned away. But you couldn't. I know that. You never back down. Simpson knows that, too. He remembers. And that's why you've got to stop him damming the creek."

"Can't be done, not the way you want," Blake said, getting to his feet and pacing back and forth beside the bench. "I saw him today. He's older, but the hate's still there. None of it's mellowed. The fightin's got to be done in a way he understands. He knows power. He respects it."

"I wish there was some other way."

"You do, I do, Dix does, but there isn't any other way. We're not fightin' some kind of crusade, Hannah. This isn't one of your King Arthur stories. It's real."

"I'm afraid they'll kill you this time."

"If they can."

"Simpson's got a lot of men. He practically owns the town."

"All my life someone's been after me, Hannah. I'm still here."

"I've missed you," she said. "I don't see how we could ever have drifted apart."

"That was Simpson's doin', too. Hannah, I never stopped lovin' you."

"It would have been better if you had," she whispered. "I've got another husband now. He's a good man, Caulie. I don't want to hurt him."

"I understand. I'm only here to stop Simpson."

"Caulie, I'm hoping you'll have a chance to get to know the boys again. They're so much like you. Zach rides like a devil, and Carter's gotten so tall. You'll hardly recognize him."

"You've done a good job with 'em then. And the little ones?" He asked, pointing to the girl in particular.

"Her name's Sally. She was five last week. The twins are Todd and Wylie. They're almost four."

"You always did want a big family."

"A ranch takes a lot of hands."

Blake laughed, remembering how she'd said the same thing years before when they'd held hands in the oak grove.

"Of course five seems enough," she said, pointing to the lines of washing hanging behind the house.

"What you want done, Hannah, won't be easy. It means startin' with the dam. Simpson might deal with you on it. More likely he'll just squeeze."

"How?"

"Block the markets. Cut your credit."

"You seem to know a lot about this."

"I've seen it before. Big ranchers never seem to be content with what they have. They want more."

"So first we bargain."

"Or try to."

"And then?"

"It's war, Hannah. We can blow the dam. Simpson can knock down fences, run off cows, and shoot the bulls. He'll try to isolate you, pick off your friends one by one."

"He'll come for you first."

"No, last. He'll want me to watch. It's you and the children that are most vulnerable. He'll go after you."

She shuddered, and he let her lean against his side. His great strong hand held her tightly, and for a second the clock moved back. It was spring and they were thirteen again. But it didn't last. She wriggled free and walked toward the door.

"I'll see what's keeping the boys," she told him.

He stepped down from the veranda and stumbled over beside the swing. He felt his eyes moisten. It's strange, he thought. How can two people who shared so much, loved each other so completely, have ever come to this? He wiped his eyes and stared out across the creek, toward the Diamond S and the town of Simpson, toward the white-haired old man who'd been the cause of so much pain.

Blake hadn't shed a tear in thirty years, not since the winter of 1850 when his mother died. At this moment he could have, possibly should have. For if all their buried dreams and grand plans for a boundless future weren't worth crying over, nothing ever would be.

A door slammed, and he shook himself out of the gloom. Two boys appeared on the steps, a tall, solid fourteen-year-old with straw-colored hair and a thin, somber-faced boy of thirteen. Blake felt his legs wobble a bit as he walked toward them. The boys stood frozen to the steps, unable or unwilling to move.

"Carter? Zach?" Blake called to them.

The eldest, Carter, nodded his head. Zach backed away a step.

"I'm your father," Blake announced.

"Our father's inside," Carter said. "You left us years ago."

"Zach?" Blake asked, reaching out for the younger boy.

"Why'd you come back?" Zach asked, moving behind his brother. "We don't need you. We don't want you."

The words cut like daggers through Blake's heart. Never had he imagined they wouldn't want him. Didn't they remember the mornings they'd spent in the pond, the long rides into the hills, the nights he'd stayed up fighting their fevers or dosing a cough?

He wanted to grab them both, hold them tight and try to explain. He longed to tell them he wanted them, he needed them. But it wasn't in him. He stepped back and stared at them. His sons. How could he tell them he'd come back to help them?

"Ma said we should see you," Carter said. "We've seen you."

Blake reached out his hand, but the boys backed away.

"I wrote," Blake mumbled. "Every birthday and each Christmas."

They stared at him with blank looks.

"I sent money, all I could spare."

"It's hard to go hunting with a Yankee greenback," Carter said. "You could've come for a visit, even a short one."

Now it was Blake's time to stand silently, searching for words. How could he explain something he himself didn't fully understand?

"How could you run from them?" Carter cried out with tearful eyes. Zach said nothing, but the smaller boy's eyes were just as moist.

"I'm not runnin' now," Blake said stiffening his spine. "Maybe after a time, you'll find a way to understand."

"Understand what?" Carter asked accusingly. "How you left without so much as a good-bye? How you never once cared enough to ride by?"

Never cared? Blake felt all the brightness, all the warmth within himself die. How many times had he stayed up wondering how they were faring, imagining what they looked like? How many sleepless nights came when a winter blizzard struck, just because he wondered if they were warm?

"I'm here now," Blake mumbled. "For what it's worth I've missed you. Maybe after the sting is gone, you'll ride out and visit a bit."

They turned their heads and returned to the house.

"They're only boys," Hannah told him afterward. "They're confused. And hurt. They'll come around."

But as Blake mounted his horse and headed for Dix's ranch, he couldn't help wondering. Forgiving came hard at thirteen or fourteen. And he wasn't able to forget the cold, hard look in their eyes.

Chapter Five

Blake reached the small gate of the Stewart ranch as the sun began its long descent into the western hills. Dix had built a wooden cabin on the place after returning from the war, but a month after he'd married Rita Thorpe, he'd moved to town and taken over the small mercantile store owned by her uncle. In the late sixties Dix had turned the store over to Rita while he'd teamed with Caulfield Blake and Martin Cabot to round up wild mustangs from the plains and break them to saddle. The army had been buying mounts then, and although the market was poor enough in town, it was as good a cash crop as corn or vegetables.

As Blake crossed the rolling hills that led to the cabin, he noticed Dix had added cattle. It wasn't much of a herd, only a scattered mixture of range cows and steers plus an occasional bull. Blake had seen a thousand like herds. All over western Texas small farms had turned their fields over to cattle. And those lucky enough to consign their stock to a large ranch in order to get them to market could make a nice enough profit. For many the cattle were destined to graze a lifetime on the scrub grasses of the plain, providing food for the family and barter for other goods in town.

As Blake paused to stare back at the ranch his father had carved out of the barren frontier landscape, he noticed a rider approaching from the west. It was a familiar sight, that lean man crouched over his horse, blazing along and shouting like a Comanche.

"Caulie!" the man screamed.

"Dix Stewart," Blake mumbled, turning his horse so as to greet his old friend.

"I knew you'd come," Dix said, fighting to catch his breath as he reined his horse to a stop. "Knew it."

"Well, you've got trouble, I hear."

"In spades, Caulie. Have you been to see Hannah yet? She's in for the worst of it, I expect."

"The creek's dryin' up."

"Simpson built a dam across Carpenter Creek just this side of Siler's Hollow."

"He must want this land bad. Has he offered you a price as of yet?"

"No."

"He's likely to wait a bit longer now."

"Oh?"

"I saw him in town. He wasn't exactly glad to see me."

"Never was too high on you, Caulie. Well, he did run you out of the county."

"No, the rest of 'em did that. Simpson could never have managed it on his own."

"And I guess we helped, Hannah and me and Marty. Can't tell you the nights I've thought about that, Caulie. It would have been so easy to step right into the middle of it."

"It wasn't your fight."

"Since when did either one of us ever have a fight without the other divin' into it?"

"You had Rita and the kids to worry after."

"That's what I told myself, Caulie, but I believe it a little less every year. And now, when Simpson's after the rest of us, you come runnin' the first time we ask."

"It was Hannah who asked."

"She'd never done it on her own. Caulie, she's just as rock stubborn as you are. That's why you came to leave, or can't you recall? Somebody should've sat down with you and made you listen."

"Nobody did, though, Dix."

"It was just plain stupid for you two to go separate ways."

"I wouldn't say she's done all that bad since I left. She's got a good man in Marsh Merritt. The ranch looks better'n ever."

"I don't catch her laughin' often, Caulie."

"Well, she's had little enough to laugh about in this life. It's been hard on her."

"Harder than on you?"

"I didn't ride out here to talk about me. Fill me in on what's been goin' on."

"Let's sit a bit. I've been ridin' all day, and I'm not young anymore. Too much shopkeepin', I suppose."

"You?" Blake said, dismounting and following Dix to a nearby oak grove. "I once remember you stayin' in the saddle thirty-six hours runnin'."

"Runnin' from Yanks. Caulie, that's been fifteen years. I don't know as I could do it now."

"I imagine you could."

"I'd hate to have my life hangin' on it. Caulie, have you seen the boys?"

"Carter and Zach?"

"You got any others? That Carter's grown another foot every time I see him. Zach's the one to watch, though. He's quiet, but that mind's always workin'. He's like you, Caulie. Rides the same, too. I swear sometimes there's a cyclone roarin' across these hills, but I look close and find out it's only Zach."

"They weren't any too glad to see me."

"Don't expect they remember you much. And they're worried about their ma. Hannah's been showin' the strain lately."

Blake frowned. The words weren't pleasant to hear. Still, she'd endured hardships before. He sat across a small pond from Dix and stared at the dying sun.

"Simpson's got no hold on us legally," Dixon said. "The deeds all spell out rights to water from Carpenter Creek. I talked to Jefferson Perry, a young lawyer out of Austin. He says we're within our rights to bust the dam."

"So, why haven't you?"

"Simpson keeps a small army up there all the time. Who is there besides Marty and me to do it? You know I never used explosives, Caulie. What we need is help with some dynamite."

"Black powder'd do it."

"Not so sure. Simpson put rocks in the foundation. It won't go easy."

"Neither did the rail bridges at Good Hope Church. It can be done."

"We may not have a choice. Perry filed papers, but somehow they got lost short of Austin. What's more, Simpson had dinner with the new land commissioner."

"So we're unlikely to get help from the authorities."

"'Bout as likely as for the old man to get hit by lightnin' eatin' his breakfast."

Blake laughed at the thought. Dix was less amused.

"Caulie, first thing we've got to do is meet with the colonel, see if we can reach an understandin'."

"Not much chance of that."

"Got to try just the same."

"And when that doesn't work?"

"Then we get serious. We can hurt Simpson as much as he can hurt us. He gets his supplies off the road that runs through the off quarter of my property. We can close that road."

"It'd take a hundred men. Anyway, he'll just cut a new road."

"That'd take time, and lots of manpower."

"Leavin' the dam open."

"And the fences. Fences are easy to cut. Cattle all over means a roundup."

"Anything else?"

"Not on our part. But there is another factor."

"Oh?"

"He's started bringin' in men. Not ranch hands. These men ride tall horses and wear Mexican spurs."

"Killers."

"And you're bound to be the first target, Caulie. Done much shootin' lately?"

"Not at people."

"You were good with a handgun once."

"Guess I'll have to be again. Tell me, Dix, have you discussed any of this with Hannah?"

"Not even with Rita. The less they know, the better."

"I agree. I think we should meet with Simpson first. Then we try a few diversions. Finally, if necessary, we blow the dam."

"How do you think it'll turn out?"

"I think we've got too few people to make it work."

"Well, the Mexicans over in Ox Hollow will pitch in. And Marty Cabot, of course. Three or four families from town, too."

"Can they fight?"

"Joe Stovall and Art Powell you remember from the war. I ordered us a case of Winchesters. That ought to even things a bit."

"People are goin' to get killed over this, Dix."

"Seems likely."

"Is it worth it?"

"If it isn't, I don't know what is. I don't make my livin' out here anymore, Caulie, but it's my land. My daddy passed it on to me, and I aim to do the same to Charlie. No fat old man's goin' to chase me off it. I never retreated from Grant, and I'll be hanged if I back down now."

"Then it's settled."

"Caulie, you plannin' to stay with Hannah?"

"I didn't feel I'd be welcome."

"Nobody stays at the cabin anymore. You're welcome to it. We've got a spare bed in town, but if it's all the same, I'd feel better havin' someone out here."

"Seems like a hard proposition to pass up."

Dix smiled, and the two old friends clasped hands in a firm shake. Then Dix excused himself. Blake watched sadly as his old friend rode toward town and his family, bound for a warmth, a sense of belonging Blake hadn't known in seven long years. It was painful to think of it.

As the gathering darkness settled in all around him, Blake rode to the cabin. He spread out his blankets on one of the two beds. The place was clean. Dix had obviously prepared for him. Then Caulie remembered he hadn't seen Rita in town. The cabin definitely showed a woman's touch.

Caulie enjoyed a light supper of boiled beef and corn bread, then readied himself for sleep. As he sat in the bed, staring out the open window at the distant light that marked the Bar Double B, he frowned. He had ridden so far, and yet he was no more at home than when he'd been in the little picket cabin on the Clear Fork of the Brazos. He sighed and closed his eyes.

No sooner had he fallen into a light slumber than he heard hoofbeats on the road. Instinctively he sat up, grabbed his revolver. He rolled off the bed and slipped over behind a great oaken chest. A horse came to a stop outside, and a lone rider entered the house.

"Who's there?" Caulie asked cautiously. "Make yourself known."

"It's just me," a young voice called out. "Zach."

The boy stepped into the moonlight streaming through the window and held his hands out to each side of his body.

"For heaven's sake, son, don't you know better'n to ride up on a man in the middle of the night?"

"It's not that late," Zach said, walking over and sitting beside his father on the bed. "'Sides, Ma wasn't eager to have me come."

"She know you're here?"

"No, sir."

"You didn't tell her?"

"I was afraid she'd be angry. She doesn't take to talking about you much. It saddens her, I think."

"And what else do you think?"

"You came 'cause she asked. I heard Ma talking to Marsh about the letter. He wasn't any too happy."

"And you?"

"I'm glad you came. People always say I'm like you. I guess it's about time I found out."

"You don't remember much from before, I guess."

"Sometimes. I remember how you took us up into the hills. And I remember the fight you had with Ma over riding to town that morning, the day you left."

"I didn't want to leave."

"Then how come you did?"

"It's not an easy thing to understand."

"Maybe that's because there really wasn't a good reason. Pa, I used to wake up in the night and think I saw you coming in to look at us, the way you did when we were little. I used to run out whenever a stranger rode up, hoping it might be you."

Blake pulled the boy over against his shoulder. Zach threw his arms around his father's shoulders and sobbed.

"I won't be disappearin' again on you, son," Blake vowed, squeezing the boy's thin shoulders. "I promise."

"Don't make any promises, Pa. They're hard to keep."

They sat together in the darkness a long time, swapping stories of hunting deer and buffalo, or riding horses and being thrown. Finally Blake stood up and pointed at the fading lights coming from the Bar Double B.

"Your ma's waitin' up on you," Blake said, pointing to a single flicker of yellow on the far horizon.

"Then I guess I better head home. Maybe I can ride night watch with you."

"What do you know of night watch?"

"Mr. Stewart told me all kinds of stories, how you raided the railroads and captured Yankee wagons."

"That was a long time ago."

"Before I was born."

"Good night, Zach. Be careful on the road home."

"I'll just climb up on old Jasper out there. He knows the trail home blindfolded, so the dark doesn't much matter."

Caulie chuckled at the boy. And watching him ride off, Caulie couldn't help feeling a father's pride.

"He'll make a fine man," Caulie said as the hoofbeats melted away into the chorus of crickets and owls. "All he needs is a little time to grow."

Lying alone on the hard oak slat bed, Caulfield Blake promised himself Zach would have that time. It would be one thing Simpson wouldn't steal.

Chapter Six

If Caulfield Blake was unsure of his reasons for returning, Zach's visit erased any doubts. Blake woke up early, took an ax from Dix's toolshed, and began splitting mesquite logs. For the briefest of times he shut out the world of trouble that was hovering above his head. He was as close to home as he'd been in years, and as he gazed out across the familiar slopes and gullies, he recalled other, better times. He set aside his ax a moment and watched the sun paint an amber swath across the hills. A moment later he trotted toward the porch and fetched a loaded Winchester.

The sound of approaching horses drifted across the landscape. At first they appeared to be coming from the Bar Double B, but now, as he concentrated, Blake realized the horsemen were arriving from the south . . . from town . . . and maybe from Henry Simpson.

"He was never one to waste time," Blake grumbled as he readied himself for the coming confrontation. As it happened, though, the lead rider was none other than Dix Stewart. With Dix rode a bewhiskered scarecrow whose scarred brow and fiery red hair betrayed him as Marty Cabot. A thin-faced man a dozen years younger trailed along behind.

"Never thought I'd live to see the day!" Marty bellowed as he rolled off his saddle and clasped Blake's hands. "Caulie, I tell you, you look fit, my friend."

"And you look like you haven't eaten in a month," Blake commented as he stepped a foot away and examined his old friend. "Ought to've married a cook instead of the prettiest hair in Wichita."

"Maybe, but I've got no complaints. Shoot, even Hannah's ma had a hard time puttin' meat on these old bones, and Emma Siler could cook the feathers off a goose."

Blake laughed as Marty tugged on a pair of suspenders. Dix interrupted then.

"Caulie, this is the fellow I was tellin' you all about," Dix said, nodding toward the stranger. "Jeff Perry's his name. He reads the law. He's a fair man with a writ, and he's the one to spell out what we're up against."

"Mr. Blake," Perry said, extending a hand. Blake shook it, then looked the young lawyer over.

"Perry? Have a brother name of Patrick?"

"Yes, sir," Perry answered. "He wrote many a letter from Tennessee with your name on it. Swore by you, Captain."

"Or at him," Marty remarked.

"Either way, it got him through the campaigns," young Perry commented.

"And just where'd Pat be nowadays?" Blake asked.

"Last I heard in the Dakotas, doing his best to get rich. You know Patrick. He never could settle down to a thing."

"Yes," Blake mumbled, knowing the same thing had been said of others.

"So, Jeff, tell it," Dix said, taking a seat on the rickety porch and motioning for the others to do likewise. Blake sat between his two old friends and waited for Perry to begin. The young lawyer paced back and forth, then suddenly pointed to the west.

"There's the trouble in a nutshell," Perry declared angrily. "It's Henry Simpson. He thinks he owns Texas."

"He does own a pretty fair chunk of it," Marty remarked.

"Not all of it, at least not yet." Perry paused long enough to brush the hair back from his forehead before continuing. "I read the deeds, even showed them to a judge in Austin. You've got clear rights to the water from Carpenter Creek. Simpson's built a hindrance to that water."

"And here I thought he'd built a dam," Marty said, laughing.

"What it means is he can't stop you from getting that water. It's a kind of a rule in law. It's the same as building a fence across a road to keep your neighbors in. He can't do it."

"Does seem like he has," Blake said sourly. "Our problem is what to do about it."

"Exactly," Perry agreed. "Normally a county judge would issue an order of sorts, but there hasn't been a county judge here for better than a year now."

"The last one sort of disappeared," Marty explained. "Some say he's gone off to Tennessee or somewhere. Heard judges have a way of gettin' shot when they go against Simpson's wishes."

"So what do we do about that?" Blake asked.

"We file papers at the state capital," Perry replied. "I've been to Austin, and I did just that. But somehow or another those papers've disappeared. I can't prove anything, of course, but it's clearly Simpson's work. He's paid off a clerk somewhere. I filed a second time, but there's no guarantee these papers won't disappear, too. It's best to do it through the courts, but . . ."

"By the time anybody does anythin', Hannah'll be long on parched corn and mighty short on cattle," Caulie grumbled, shaking his head. "You, too, Dix. At least the Bar Double B's got a fair stretch of the Colorado for its northern boundary."

"And my place has got no water to speak of," Marty complained. "I always run my cattle over on Dix's range in the dry season. Now what am I to do? A spring and a pond may provide for the family, but my stock'll be dead inside a month."

"Well, I've got to give it to Simpson," Caulie said, rising to his feet. "He's come up with a fine notion of how to grab half a county. To think Hannah's ma sold him his first acre, and my pa helped frame his barn! Well, any dam that can get built can also be blown to perdition. Bedford Forrest taught me that much."

"You haven't been down there," Dix argued. "You don't know. Simpson expects that. He's got men waitin', eager to ambush anybody who sets foot on that dam. There are always three or four of 'em up there, and they carry their guns loose and easy, like they know what they're about."

"We've dealt with worse," Blake said, laughing. "Why, I remember we rode through half a regiment of Ohio cavalry back in Tennessee, and they were nothin' to those Comanches back in 'sixty-six."

"That was a long time ago," Dix reminded Blake. "We were young. The most I ride anymore's from here to town and back. I've got responsibilities, too. So does Marty."

"So what will you do, sell out?"

"To my knowledge, Simpson isn't making any offers," Perry said, shuffling some papers into a small valise. "I don't see you have any choice. Destroy that dam or . . ."

"Give up?" Blake asked. "Not on your life. I've never been much good at surrenderin'. Tell you what, Jefferson Perry. You keep filin' those papers of yours down in Austin. Go to Washington if you have to. As long as Simpson knows you're tryin', he's apt to ease his guard a bit. Meanwhile . . ."

"Yes?" Dix asked.

"We'll round everybody up, have a talk. And who knows? Some dark night when the moon's all gone, an old rebel might just ride down and pay a visit on Henry Simpson's dam. Could be that rebel just might take a couple of Texas candles along with him."

"Texas candles?" Perry asked.

"Dynamite," Marty explained as he threw his hat in the air. "Whoopee! Caulie, I'm glad you came back. Don't know how much good you'll do with this, but you sure make things interestin'."

Blake received a somewhat different response later that morning when Dix Stewart led the way to Ox Hollow. It was hard to imagine a more miserable stretch of farmland anywhere in creation. Boulders three feet tall peppered every hillside, and gullies etched the sandy soil as if some giant hawk had clawed the ground in anger. The few trees were mostly scrub mesquite or gnarled junipers, good for little save fenceposts and stove wood. And yet a half-dozen Mexican families managed to eke out a living planting vegetables and a few acres of sweet corn.

The men, including a pair of boys who couldn't have reached fourteen, listened as Dix and Jeff Perry explained their plans. The farmers listened in grim silence. Finally a thin-faced man stepped forward.

"Yes, yes," the farmer said, clearly unconvinced. "Excuse me, but your plans have nothing to say to me and my family. We have no water from Carpenter Creek. Your papers will do nothing for us. We don't have thirsty cows. We have starving children.

"Not so long ago we spoke to you when men came and burned the fields of our cousins on the Colorado River. You did nothing. Now others come and shoot at our little ones. What will you do about this? I tell you. Nothing. You look for help in the wrong place."

"It's Simpson sends those night riders," Dix objected. "If we band together . . ."

"Ah, this always sounds so good," a second farmer broke in. "We are always promised help. And what price do we pay? Our blood. We fight for our land. We die if we must. But we will not ride with you."

Dix started to argue, but Blake pulled him away.

"He's right," Blake said. "I know these men. Shoot, Roberto Salazar there helped me drive my first longhorns to market. His pa taught me to rope mustangs. Now, when they settle out here on their own, the same men who promised them a better life stand by and watch Simpson do his best to run 'em off."

"Yes, we remember you, too," Roberto said, emerging from the others. "You know my brother Hernando, though he has been away as long a time as you."

The thin-faced man nodded, and Blake smiled. Hernando had

never been one to back away from a fight, and the two had tangled once or twice in younger years.

"My wife," Caulie began, coughing as he realized Hannah now shared another man's life. "My wife and her ma sold this land to your father." Caulie continued speaking to the two men with watery eyes. "Your ma helped birth my boys, and it was no easy thing bringin' that pair of howlin' coyotes into this life, believe you me. I'm not askin' you to ride anywhere. I'm just sayin' we've got common cause now as we once did when Comanches did their best to ride us all into the dust. Your papa stood at my elbow the day we killed Little Wolf.

"I'm not makin' a speech or anythin', just remindin' you it wasn't me told you lies. Whatever happens at Carpenter Creek, you know Henry Simpson's bound to call here first. You're closer, for one thing. For another, he's had an eye on this range for years. Emma Siler sold it to old Arturo more to spite Simpson than anythin' else."

"We know," Hernando said, producing an old flintlock musket. "We will be ready."

"Well, you'll accomplish little with that," Caulie said. "You may not think my words mean much, but Dix has ordered a case of Winchester repeaters. Make one man into ten. I'll see how many I can talk him out of for you."

"We have no money to pay . . ."

"I didn't say anythin' about selling, did I?" Caulie asked, grinning. "An old friend can make you a loan, can't he? You'll return them when you've finished."

"I don't take . . ." Hernando began.

"Take?" Caulie asked. "Lord, I've still got a poncho of yours someplace, Hernando. I remember pullin' cactus thorns out of your backside. You borrowed my pants. Don't tell me you're particular about whose rifle you fire!"

"I promise we'll use them to good effect," Roberto said, clasping Caulie's hand. "You should never have let them drive you off, amigo. Old man Simpson has had the run of the range too long."

"We'll just have to run him down like a renegade mustang. You keep your eyes sharp, old friends. Simpson hasn't been collectin' shooters out there for the hang of it."

"Yes, he hates us plenty," Hernando agreed. "But I never hung his son. You watch out yourself, Caulfield Blake. Some of these fellows Simpson has hired have the eyes of an owl. They shoot real well in the dark."

"I'll keep that in mind," Caulie promised as he turned away. He motioned for Dix and Jeff Perry to follow.

"All the way over here I was sorry we left Marty at his place," Dix grumbled "Bein' a neighbor, he has better luck with 'em. That Hernando's a hard case."

"Maybe," Caulie grumbled. "But I'd be happy to have him with me in a tight spot. He's right about one thing, Dix. He won't be runnin'. Get 'em some of those Winchesters. They'll put 'em to good use."

"I'll do it straightaway."

"I think it's time for me to head south," Perry declared, glancing at his pocket watch. "I'll leave the horse at the livery, Dix. With luck, I'll catch the three o'clock coach to Austin."

"Jeff, you keep out of trouble's shadow. It's dangerous work sidin' with us," Caulie warned the young lawyer.

"I've known tight corners before, Mr. Blake. You leave me to find my way home."

Caulie couldn't help smiling. Dix had certainly chosen the right friends. Somehow the odds didn't look so bleak as before.

"Dix, you'll be headin' to town yourself, won't you? Maybe it'd be best if you go along now. I don't favor the thought of either one of you ridin' alone past the Diamond S."

"So what'll you be doin'?"

"Takin' a ride out Simpson's way."

"To Carpenter Creek?"

"Scoutin' the lay of the land, you might say. I once was a fair Indian scout, remember?"

"It's you best do the rememberin', Caulie Blake. Think back to how that piece of flint got hammered into your hip. Bullet can make a bigger hole, and there are those up that way who'd be paid well for closin' your eyes."

"Others have tried," Caulie said, spitting at a small, withered corn plant. "I won't make it that easy for 'em."

He watched Dix and Perry ride. In truth Caulfield Blake would have felt easier with Dix Stewart at his side, but by now word of Blake's return would be out. Anyone riding with a hunted man shared the peril, and besides, Caulie had grown accustomed to solitude.

From the broken hills north of Ox Hollow, Caulie followed the Diamond S fence line past Marty Cabot's ramshackle cabin and weathered barn. Marty'd never been one to slap paint on lumber, but the place seemed in a worse way than ever. Except for a few chickens out past the barn and a pair of mares in a rail corral, the ranch was deserted.

"Likely Marty's out workin' the stock," Caulie told himself. Even so, that didn't explain where Eve and the little ones had gone. There were two little boys. The oldest had barely been walking when Caulie'd left. Three daughters had followed, one a year from '75 on. Hannah had written back in '78 that Eve had lost the two youngest to winter, though she was now in the family way again.

Lord, Caulie thought. Marty Cabot's got kids I've never seen. Who would have dreamed it possible when the two of them were boys, chasing jackrabbits through the creek bottoms and alternately pestering Hannah Siler and asking her for favors? But then who would have believed Caulfield Blake could ever ride away?

"You did that to me, Simpson!" Caulfield suddenly cried. And with ill-concealed rage, he drew out a rope, formed a loop, and threw it over the nearest fencepost. As the frail mesquite wood cracked and splintered, Caulie grinned bitterly. He had more in store for Henry Simpson than tearing down a few fenceposts.

Caulie crossed the market road, then tore down a six-foot section of fence a mile and a half south of Carpenter Creek. He managed to locate the splices in the barbed wire and separate them. He then wound the loose strands of the devilish wire around the remaining posts so that the gap was safe for riders.

"No point to layin' open your feet with those barbs, huh?" Caulie whispered as he stroked the lathered neck of his ebony stallion. "You may have need of those feet, boy. We're not exactly ridin' onto friendly ground now."

The horse shuddered, and Caulie stroked the animal's flanks. He'd ridden the stallion long and hard from the Clear Fork, and the wear was beginning to show. He told himself to ease the pace for a few days.

It didn't take long for Caulie to tell this was Simpson land. Cattle ran everywhere. Soon it was possible to see the new lake that flooded Siler's Hollow. Several hundred head watered in the nearby meadows. Caulie ignored them. His eyes focused on the dam.

It was more substantial than he first thought. Most dams were formed by piling logs up, then adding long stems of buffalo grass, rock, and sand until a wall of sorts formed. Soon debris and mud accumulated, and the water flow was halted. During the war Forrest's cavalry had often blasted such makeshift dams to bits with a keg or two of powder. Simpson's dam appeared to be of rock. Worse, it was close to ten feet thick. A little dynamite might produce a hole or two if planted deep, but that would require a block of time. The three dark-browed gunmen patrolling the dam seemed unlikely to offer any help.

"You never in your whole life made it simple, did you, old man?" Caulie asked. "It was a dark day when your ma birthed you, Henry Simpson."

But Caulfield Blake hadn't taken on many easy jobs. Hannah never would have written if times hadn't been desperate. Caulie took a deep breath, exhaled, then nudged his horse into a trot. As he emerged from cover, the guards on the dam shouldered their rifles.

"Hold up there!" Caulie yelled. "I come alone—and in peace."

"Peace?" a heavy voice bellowed out. "What right have you

got to peace? Blake, you're on my land. I'd be within my rights to shoot you dead!"

Caulie glared as Henry Simpson rode out past his guards and galloped the fifty feet to where Caulfield Blake sat atop his tall black. The two old enemies stared at each other. There wasn't a hint of forgiving in either man's eyes.

"I've come to speak of the dam, Simpson," Caulie finally said.

"Oh?"

"You want to talk about rights. When Emma Siler deeded you this range, she made it clear who had rights to Carpenter Creek."

"Why don't you hire yourself a lawyer?" Simpson asked, laughing to himself. "You once got my boy hung. Maybe you can get my dam broken down the same way."

"I didn't hang anybody," Caulie said bitterly. "Austin did the killin', and that was your doin', Simpson. If anybody's to be held account . . ."

"Enough!" Simpson screamed with blazing eyes. "The dam stays. I'll choke that creek till the buzzards pick at all that's left of you, Blake, and your whole accursed family. I'll see you cry for your boys the way I have for mine."

"You cry?" Caulie asked. "I never saw any tears. You built yourself a reputation on the graves of Matt and Henry, two men who might've made fair soldiers if they hadn't listened to their pa's tales of leadin' charges and dyin' in glory. Then you used Austin to burn out your neighbors, to kill those who got in the way. When the law stilled your hand, you turned the people against me and mine. Well, the shame belongs to me for lettin' it happen, for stayin' quiet back then. I've had a lot of years to think it over, and I'm through playin' it your way. If you think you can hurt me or mine, you're mistaken. Won't be my blood spilled this time around. No, sir."

"I wouldn't be so sure," Matt Simpson said as he led a half-dozen rifle-toting men down from the dam. "You can't fight the whole world single-handed, Blake, You were mighty fierce in town with a sheriff's shotgun nearby. Care to try your hand out here?"

Matt strode forward with a swagger. His arrogant grin and jaunty step reminded Caulfield Blake of other youngsters, poor cowboys who'd spent a year's trail money on fancy spurs and a tall hat. The Colt revolvers which might have won them respect never cleared their holsters. The dark-eyed veterans calmly, coldly killed each and every one.

Caulie laughed, then motioned at the surrounding countryside.

"Blakes and Silers settled this country," he shouted. "When the world was young, my pa was battlin' Comanches and rattlers out here along the Colorado. You, Simpson, came along when the worst of it was over. You spin your tales and make up your history. *Colonel* Simpson? What regiment did you ever lead? You passed the whole war in your rockin' chair, and you didn't raise an eyebrow when the Yanks won. No, you didn't even complain about the garrisons or the Ohio judges till they raised your taxes. Even then, you were better off than most.

"You, Matt Simpson. Ever ask your grandpa how I come to wear a badge? Was Henry Simpson handed it to me. Was that old man there who sent me out to bring Austin in ahead of the cavalry. He thought the trail could be bought."

"You're lying!" young Simpson yelled, riding out in front of the others. A pair of bucksin-clad companions followed. Caulie knew both from a run-in back at The Flat. Abe and Noah Jenkins had a reputation for drawing quick and shooting straight. Neither asked many questions other than how much gold a killing might put in a pocket.

"So that's how it's to be, is it?" Caulie asked, yawning. "Seems a bit early for a showdown. You Jenkins boys usually prefer your fightin' after dusk, I hear."

"Calm down, Matt," Henry Simpson urged. "We've barely begun our game."

"You mean to let his words stand, Grandpa?" Matt asked.

"Nobody's heard 'em," Simpson declared. "You boys know a lie at its face, don't you?"

The men on the dam laughed nervously. Caulie tensed. Abe Jenkins ran his fingers along the barrel of a Colt.

"You heard him," Matt said in disgust. "Get back to your work." The Jenkins brothers turned away. Then Matt pointed to Blake and cried, "It's not finished. Just postponed. I'll be coming for you."

"I'm not hard to find," Caulie responded. "But you make sure you do your prayin' first 'cause there's not apt to be time after. You hear?"

"I haven't heard a word you've said since I met you," Matt said, laughing loudly. "Now get off our land!"

A rifle barked from the dam, and a single bullet split the air to Caulie's left. Slowly, cautiously, Caulie turned and rode away. The day would come when he'd have to settle with Matt Simpson, but that could wait. The odds weren't favorable at present.

Chapter Seven

As evening shadows settled upon the land, Caulie made a second visit to Simpson's dam. Under the cloak of night he crawled along the creekbed until he was within ten feet of the dam itself. The guards huddled around a small fire and sang camp songs as they gazed out across the valley. Their eyes searched for men on horseback, though, and they failed to detect the lone shadow, that ghost of a man crawling along the dying stream below.

Caulie examined the dam as carefully as he could without risking discovery. Even blowing a small hole in the stone surface would be no easy task. A solitary man couldn't creep in and plant explosives. He would need help.

He studied the structure for a moment before slipping back into the cover of nearby boulders. Three charges set near the base of the dam might crack the rock wall. The force of the water backed up in Siler's Hollow would likely do the rest. If not, he'd better convince Hannah to leave.

He led his horse back through the tangle of briars and scrub mesquite that covered the broken country south of Carpenter

Creek. He didn't mount up until he was a quarter mile off. Then he rode briskly toward the gap he'd torn in the Diamond S fence abutting Dix Stewart's place. From the fence it was less than two miles on to Dix's cabin. He was there almost before he knew it. After seeing to his horse, he took out a yellowing sketch pad from his saddlebags and penciled in the dam, the creek, what cover he'd located, and which paths might offer escape.

Caulie knew Simpson's men would have the wire mended by the time Dix and the others would be ready to move against the dam. The best way out would be along the creek, toward Hannah's place, or else straight into town. Taking the creek would be tricky, what with a wall of water raging down on them once the dam burst. But the route to town led past the Simpson ranch buildings, and no one crossing the Diamond S after the explosion could expect a friendly greeting.

The following morning Caulie met with Marty and Dix at the cabin. The three old friends pored over the rough map, then argued about the plan.

"You know this is like touchin' off a powder keg under old man Simpson," Dix said, scratching his head. "It'll mean open war."

"Hasn't it come to that already?" Caulie asked. "Water out here's life."

"He could send riders over to Hannah's place," Dix pointed out. "It could get really rough. Who's goin' with us anyway?"

"Us?" Caulie asked. "It's certain you can't come."

"Nothin' short of death would stop me," Dix declared. "I always rode at your side when General Forrest had somethin' of this sort in mind."

"Not this time, Dix. If you leave town, someone's bound to take note. If it doesn't tip Simpson, you're sure to catch the blame once it's done. This way you can invite somebody over, maybe sup with the minister or the sheriff."

"Caulie's right," Marty agreed. "But that argument hardly applies to me. I can slip away anytime I care to, and nobody's the wiser. Shoot, I stay out on the range three nights out of four in the summer. All that wailin' of the little ones drives me to drink."

"You'd best change that habit," Caulie said, frowning. "Once trouble starts, you'll want Eve to have somebody around."

"She will, Caulie. Caleb and Court'll be there. That Caleb's close to as fine a shot at ten as you were."

"This isn't shootin' turkeys, Marty. There'll be dyin'. I wouldn't want Carter or Zach facin' those Jenkins brothers."

"You know about that, do you?"

"We had a disagreement last year up at The Flat. Seems Abe was playin' with his sleeves when he should've been dealin' top cards."

"You must've mellowed some, Caulie," Dix observed. "Time was you shot card sharks."

"They mostly get themselves hung, but we had the money, and I guess we considered that satisfactory. Wish I'd known then I'd wander across those two again down here. Might've saved some trouble."

"Simpson'd only've hired himself another pair," Dix said, angrily staring out the door toward the Diamond S. "One thing Texas hasn't been short of since the war's men long on shootin' talents and short on cash money. And that doesn't take into account all the renegade bluecoats run off from the army posts or the washed-up buffalo hunters."

"No," Caulie agreed. "Next thing is to get hold of some dynamite. We'll need fuse, too. Five to ten minute lengths. Three charges ought to get the job done. Marty and I can set 'em. We'll need a third fellow to tend the horses and watch our rear."

"I'll speak to Hernando," Marty offered. "He's steady."

"No," Dix objected. "Anybody leaves Ox Hollow, a dozen folks'll know. Better to speak to Joe Stovall. I use him sometimes on the ranch. I can send him out toward dusk, say he's gone to mend fence or look to the stock."

"Then as soon as you get me the dynamite, we're ready," Caulie said, grinning grimly. "The rest is up to you."

"I'll get the dynamite to Marty. You'll be set to go tomorrow night?"

Caulie nodded, then led his friends to the door.

He thought to make a third and final scout of the dam that next afternoon, but he'd scarcely left the cabin when he came upon Abe Jenkins and a young cowboy.

"Should've known you'd be nearby," Jenkins remarked. "We've been havin' a lot of trouble with clipped wire and broken fenceposts. Wouldn't have any notion as to how such a thing might've happened, would you, Blake?"

"Nary a one," Caulie answered. "I would mention you're not on Diamond S range now. This stretch of range belongs to Dixon Stewart. You're trespassin'."

"As I'd suspect you have been. Stay clear of Mr. Simpson's property. We've got good eyes, and they're mainly lookin' out for you. I saw the way you looked at the dam the other day. You got any idea to raid that place, best lose it. We keep watch there all night."

"What business would I have at a dam? It's enough of a job keepin' track of all the stock."

"You mark my words, Blake. Me, I'd as soon settle it right here and now, but Mr. Simpson says we're to be patient. I can be patient as Moses when the need arises. Just you remember what I said about the dam."

"Man'd be a fool to argue, Abe."

"Sure would!" Jenkins shouted. "And he'd wind up dead."

Caulfield Blake passed the remainder of the afternoon at the cabin. He kept his rifle handy lest Abe Jenkins or some other fool decided to pay a call. Two miles wasn't much distance from Simpson's gunmen. But Dix's cabin stood atop a hill, and a man could see down toward Carpenter Creek. Caulie couldn't help feeling better knowing he stood between the Diamond S and Hannah.

Shortly before dusk Marty Cabot rode up. With him was a slim-shouldered rider whose dusty leather hat concealed his face.

"This isn't any Joe Stovall," Caulie complained at once. "What in heaven's name . . ."

He never finished. A nervous hand removed the hat, and Caulie discovered Marty's companion was none other than Zach.

"Guess I'm not much of a replacement, huh?" the boy asked as he read his father's disappointment. "Simpson had a man in town watchin' Joe and Dix both. I was in town fetchin' Ma some sugar. Was bound this way anyway, so Dix sent word with me."

"She doesn't know you're here?" Caulie asked. "Well, that's just fine. Get along home with you now, boy. This isn't goin' to be a good place to be on toward dark."

"I know about the dam, Pa," Zach said, placing a stubborn hand on each hip. "I've never fought a war, but I can hold horses just fine. I know that country, too. Carter and I've been ridin' Carpenter Creek since, well, since you were here yourself."

Caulie frowned. Again he remembered how long a time it had been. But he smiled, too. There was grit in young Zach, and the boy's stringy, unkempt walnut hair reminded Caulie of his own.

"He's good with horses, Caulie," Marty declared. "I wouldn't've brought him along if I could've found anybody else. Simpson's got riders everywhere."

"Don't you think I know that?" Caulie asked. "They won't be asleep tonight. There's apt to be shootin'. Somebody . . . could get killed."

The two old cavalrymen gazed sadly at young Zach, but the thirteen-year-old would have none of it. He brushed back his hair, stroked his bay's neck, and grinned.

"It's my home, too, Pa. Maybe more'n yours. I've passed my whole life here. Besides, you need me. There's nobody else."

"He's right," Marty agreed.

"Looks like I'm outvoted. You do as you're told, though, son. There are enough Blakes buried in this country. Your time's not up for years yet."

"Yes, sir," Zach said as he slapped the dust out of his hat. "I won't let you down, Pa."

Marty and Zach dismounted and tied their horses to the porch rail. The three of them then collected around a fire and watched the sun fade as Caulie fried a tin of beans and some jerked beef. It wasn't much of a supper, and Caulie could see his guests were a bit disappointed. It was hard for a man accustomed to a woman's touch to satisfy himself with dried beef and tinned beans.

Once darkness had settled in, Caulie hauled a bucket of well water over and muddied a bit of earth. He then painted his companion's faces. Marty did Caulie's the same way.

"Next thing is to make sure you've got not a flicker of white or yellow to your outfit," Caulie explained as he looked over the horses. The he turned his attention to Zach. The boy was soon rid of a white cotton shirt and a yellow kerchief. "Can't do much about the bay, but I trust she'll keep to the trees. You can wear this old poncho of mine," Caulie went on, tossing Zach a weathered garment of black canvas. "Once we head out, ride low, bent over so you appear to be part of your horse."

"That how you did it in the war, Pa?" Zach asked.

"Long before that," Caulie said, laughing as he recalled watching with wonder at the way Comanche raiders could close to disappear on horseback.

"It's time," Marty announced finally. "We'd best get to it before moonrise. I'd not care to hand over our little packages without a bit of cover from those trigger-happy fools atop the dam."

Caulie nodded, then mounted his black stallion and led the way toward Carpenter Creek.

He wouldn't dare force the fence line anywhere near the dam. After all, the Jenkins brothers were famous for setting ambushes. And riding along the creekbed was the natural, expected approach, so Henry Simpson would never expect them to try it. Even so, Caulie had his right hand gently resting on the cold walnut handle of his Colt revolver.

The three riders rode as one as they wound their way past the barbed wire and splashed into the muddy remnant of Carpenter Creek.

"We won't be able to come back this way," Marty whispered. "The whole stretch of creek'll be flooded."

"Wish I could've warned Ma," Zach grumbled.

"Shhh," Caulie urged. "Once it's done, we'll deal with things as they are. We haven't got any dynamite planted as of yet."

The others nodded, and Caulie led on. The three rode silently up the creek bank and onward through the tangled wilderness beyond. None of them emitted so much as a sigh. Noise brought attention, and discovery meant swift and certain death. Fortunately Simpson's riders were elsewhere. Caulie reached the dam unseen. He then dismounted, helped Marty take out the dynamite charges, and watched young Zach gather the horses' reins.

Father and son exchanged a nervous glance. Caulie then touched his son on the shoulder, allowing the boy to lean on the father he scarcely knew. Then Caulie headed toward the boulders above the creek and left Zach to await their return.

Three guards paced back and forth atop the dam. No one guarded the streambed, though, and that was Caulie's destination.

"Remember, we've got to light the fuses together," Marty whispered as the two of them cowered behind the rocks. "There isn't but a few minutes before the whole thing goes. Hide the fuse as well as you can. Sparks can be seen half a mile on this kind of night."

Caulie grinned a grim acknowledgment, then darted out into the open. His feet made only the slightest sound as he tread Indian-style toward the embankment. Once safely there, he began digging in the rock. Marty soon wove his way to the far side of the creek and began placing the second charge. The two of them worked feverishly. Any second someone might notice. Caulie then carefully wedged his fuse between rocks or covered it with loose stone. He then repeated the labor and placed the final three sticks of dynamite near the dam's center.

Marty raised a hand, and Caulie lit the first fuse. He then raced for the other fuse and lit it as well. The sound of feet tramping toward the boulders attracted the guards, and one fired off a shot. Soon a half-dozen men hurried toward the dam. More shots followed. Orders bellowed across the hollow.

"Somethin's burnin'!" a guard cried out. "Powder!"

By then Caulie was dragging Marty toward the horses. Zach held the reluctant animals steady. The two raiders joined the boy just as the first explosion split the evening asunder.

"Let's get out of here," Caulie urged as he grabbed his reins and fought to mount the rearing stallion. Marty had no easier time getting atop his animal. Zach held on to his bay for dear life. The second and third charges went off together, and the air was suddenly full of spray and debris. The ground trembled. Then the water began eating its way through the dam, and what had been a muddy stretch of sand became a raging torrent.

"We did it," Zach cried, slapping his father's back.

"And now we'd better get out of here," Caulie said as he turned the big black and drove the horse forward. The dam's right side collapsed, and the water was soon eating away the left. Guards fired wildly, and men alternately issued curses and orders.

Caulie gazed for a final time at the chaos behind him. And as a wall of water swept down Siler's Hollow, scattering cattle and horsemen like leaves in the autumn breeze, it looked as if they'd just get clear. Simpson's riders had no time to chase anybody. They were scurrying for their lives.

Caulie tore through the fence line a quarter mile from his original break. He sent Marty flying homeward, then led Zach toward the cabin.

"Care for some company?" Zach asked as he pulled his bay alongside his father. "Ma's accustomed to me passin' the night over at the Cabot place on my way back from town."

"Your ma's goin' to need your help, what with the floodwaters and all."

"She won't miss me. Marsh'll do most of it, and Carter's there."

"I won't claim you wouldn't be welcome company, son, but she'll worry, you know. What's more, she won't be fond of the notion you rode with us tonight."

"I thought . . . I mean . . . I guessed maybe once I proved to you I could handle a job, you'd want me along."

Caulie pulled up short and swallowed a sudden sadness.

"You never once had anythin' to prove to me, Zach. I'm glad you're here just now, and I'd have you with me from now on if it were just the two of us that were concerned. But there's your ma to consider. I won't bring her grief and worry again. Not for anythin'. Now get along home. There'll be other days to pass together. I promise you that."

"You're back to stay then?"

"I'm back. Let's leave it at that."

"All right," Zach said, reluctantly turning his horse homeward. "Before long you'd best come out to . . . to Marsh's place . . . to home. Ma can't blow up a dam, but she's surely a better cook than you are."

Caulie laughed as the boy rode away. It was hard watching the night swallow up Zach, and the silence that ate at Caulfield Blake as he rode back to Dix's cabin was deafening. He longed for sounds, for laughter and singing. He longed for the family that had somehow slipped away. And more than ever he was determined to keep them safe.

Chapter Eight

Caulfield Blake spent an uneasy night following the destruction of Simpson's dam. Sounds of galloping horses and rampaging cattle mixed with the eerie noises of the creek eating away at its banks, tearing at rocks and hills and trees as it surged toward the distant Colorado River. By daybreak the worst of the flooding had ebbed, and all that remained was the waiting.

"Life teaches a man patience," old Calvin Blake had taught Caulie in what now seemed to have been another lifetime. "Waters rise and fall. Seasons come and go. The land survives. The trick is to outlast storm and drought, learn to take each in your stride."

Caulie had done his best, but Henry Simpson had ensured it wasn't enough.

Now it was Simpson's turn to pay. Siler's Hollow had gone from a lake to a swamp, and the frothing water unleashed by the dam had spilled over ten acres of prime grazing land. Cattle, suddenly surprised by the flood, had scrambled to high ground, trampling anything in their path. Those that had been a trifle slow had drowned by the dozens, and dead steers and cows dotted the range.

Downstream at the Bar Double B, cattle that only a day before had fought over the sandy banks of the Colorado now drank from the sweet surface of Carpenter Creek. Some trees had been uprooted by the floodwaters, and one field was awash, but the precious peach orchard had weathered the raging waters rather well, and the house, being atop a hill, was scarcely bothered.

Hannah knew even before Zach arrived that the dam had been blown. Why wouldn't she? Wasn't it for that very reason that she'd written the letter, called Caulfield Blake back? And now, as she stood on the crest of the hill with Marshall Merritt—her husband—she was less sure of her actions.

"I welcome the water," Marsh told her, "but little good will come of this. The place to fight was in a courtroom."

"Some things can't be settled that way," Hannah objected. "Dix tried that a month ago. Six months or six years, the case never would've come to trial so long as Henry Simpson wished it otherwise."

"I saw Zachary ride in last night. His face was painted dark, and he wore a black poncho . . . the kind Caulfield used to wear when he was sheriff."

"You're wrong," she declared. "Zach went into town for me. He gave me the sugar. He would never have . . ."

"Hannah, I've done my best to be a father to those boys, but Zach's never taken me to heart like Carter. Everybody says it. Zach's a Blake. It can't be changed by his taking my name."

"There's no disgrace in being a Blake, Marsh. Blakes built this place, built this county. For all his faults, Caulie never gave me cause to think poorly of his name or his family."

"I wish you'd never written that letter."

"We'd've starved, Marsh. You're a good man, and you've been as fine a father and husband as there is in Texas. But you and Dix and Marty and the others . . . you could never square off with Simpson."

"I never backed away from a fight, Hannah," Marsh said, his face growing bright scarlet. "You seem to think I'm not up to it."

"Not to beatin' Simpson, Marsh. To beat that old snake you need somebody who's not tied to the rules. Caulie will do what's necessary, no matter who comes to harm."

"I thought that's why you asked him to leave."

"It is. Back then I needed a husband, a man who'd stand by me, be there for the little ones. But just now we need Caulfield Blake, and I'm glad he's here."

"So'm I," Zach said, joining them. "You should've seen him, Ma. He was everything Dix ever said. I rode with 'em."

"You what!" she cried.

"Had to. They needed somebody to hold the horses. Ma, he rides like a general, all stiff and straight in the saddle. He's got a way . . . like nothin' can hurt him. He misses us, too. I could tell."

"He could've gotten you killed, Zach!" Hannah complained. "I can't imagine why you agreed to . . ."

"I asked to go," Zach explained. "He argued against it. Said you'd never abide it."

"He was right about that!" she thundered.

"But I remember you tellin' Carter and me how you once shouldered a musket and helped Grandma fight off a bunch of Comanches out here when you were just twelve. I figure if you could do that, I'm old enough to do my part, too."

"You should have ridden over and told your father," Hannah said, nodding toward Marshall. "When your granny and I did that, the men were miles away. And remember, we didn't go looking for those Comanches."

"Ma, I . . ."

"We'll talk no more of it, Zachary. Go help your brothers with the horses."

"Yes'm," the boy said, turning dejectedly away and starting for the corral.

Hannah watched Zach kick rocks out of his way. He was Caulie, all right, a wild mustang straining to break free. She would never hold him, not with the world out there whispering in his ear, calling him off to try his hand at this and that.

"They grow faster'n summer weeds, don't they?" Marsh asked. "Wasn't so long ago I could carry Zach and Carter, the both of 'em, around on my back. Now look at 'em! By late summer they'll be lookin' me in the eye."

"You think I was too short with him."

"I never said that, Hannah."

"But it's in your eyes."

"I think it's your place to do what you think best."

"But you'd handle it differently."

"Are you askin' me?"

"Yes."

"Then I'll go ahead and throw in my two cents worth. The boy barely knows his father."

"*You're* his father."

"I don't think so. Not after last night. Likely we made a mistake givin' those boys my name. They've a right to their father, to his name and his character. Carter, well, he's different, but Zach could hardly act otherwise."

"He's in such a hurry to be a man."

"Texas hurries 'em along. Hannah, Matt Simpson's not much older'n Carter. Like it or no, the boys're in this mess. After last night, there'll be no peace. Simpson's bound to hit back. He hasn't hired all that new help to drive longhorns to market."

"I know, and it worries me."

"Little point to worrying over it," Marsh said, taking her hand and leading the way to the house. "What's bound to happen will. We'll face it when it comes."

Even as Marshall Merritt was speaking, Henry Simpson was at work. Cowboys were rounding up the survivors of his herd while a few men set about tending to the grim task of skinning and disposing of the dead animals. Meanwhile a third band, led by young Matt and the Jenkins brothers, set off toward Ox Hollow. Marty Cabot saw them pass. Soon others were riding.

"Ma, somebody's comin'," Zach cried as he raced toward the house.

"Stay inside, Hannah," Marsh instructed as he took a Winchester rifle down from the mantel. "I'll see to this."

Hannah stood at the front window and watched him go. It might have been more prudent to pull the shutters to, but she didn't. Instead she opened a small chest and drew out an aging Colt revolver. Caulfield Blake had carried that gun once. She now considered it a kind of legacy.

"Howdy, Marsh," Marty called down as he reached the house. "Good to see you still in high spirits, Zach. We've got some trouble, my friends."

"Simpson?" Marsh asked.

"In spades. He's sent his boys after the Mexicans down in Ox Hollow. They crossed my range maybe an hour ago. I already sent Caulie out that way. I thought maybe you and . . ."

"That's not really our affair, Marty," Marsh argued. "They're way to the south. I can't very well leave Hannah and the little ones to themselves."

"And if we let him, Simpson'll ride each one of us into the dust. We can't take turns, Marsh. We've got to stand together. Dix got some rifles down to those folks, so they're apt to give a fair account of themselves. If a half-dozen of us plus a few from town pitch in, we'll give Simpson's boys somethin' to remember. Bloody 'em up proper."

"Was this Caulie's idea?" Hannah asked, stepping out onto the porch. "He sent you, did he?"

"As I recall, Hannah, it was you did the sendin'," Marty answered angrily. "Your own ma got those people settled out there. Now they're in trouble. Well, Marsh? You comin' or not? I've ridden all the way up here to fetch you. If you're not ridin' with me, it's best I'm off."

"Marsh?" Zach asked.

Hannah noticed the pain in Marsh's eyes. Always before it had been "Pa" or "Papa" when Zach spoke to Marshall Merritt. Somehow she sensed that would never happen again.

"Tell Carter to help you saddle the horses," Marsh said. "He'd best come along as well."

"He won't like that much," Zach warned.

"Maybe, but he'll do it," Marsh answered gruffly. "It's time we start pulling together, whether we call ourselves Merritts or Blakes or whatever."

Caulfield Blake waited for them on the banks of Carpenter Creek.

"Pa, we've come!" Zach shouted as he raced the bay up alongside his father's big black. "Got my rifle and everything."

"Might be best if the boys stayed out of this," Caulie said as he read the eagerness in Zach's eyes. Carter rode more reluctantly in the rear.

"It's better they get a taste of it now, in the daylight," Marsh declared. "Besides, Zach's already been in it up to his eyeballs."

"That wasn't my idea," Caulie said, leading the way south-ward toward Ox Hollow. "If it's to be, though, keep to cover, boys. Zach, you stick to my side like fleas on a hound. Carter, you . . ."

"I'll stay with my father," Carter said angrily. "He doesn't run out on people."

"Hush, boy!" Marty said angrily.

"Leave it be," Caulie said, trying to shake off the sting. "He's got a right to his feelin's."

"And good reason for them," Carter added.

"You best save all that anger for old man Simpson," Marty warned. "Pretty soon he's liable to be shootin' bullets at you. Then we'll find out who sticks and who doesn't."

Carter whirled his horse around so that Marsh lay between himself and the others. Caulie motioned Marty up front, then urged the ebony stallion into a gallop. Soon the little company raced across the broken hills at a fair pace. In an hour's time they'd crossed the road, joined up with Dix Stewart and a handful of riders from town, and were nearing Ox Hollow.

The sound of gunfire just ahead led Caulie to turn cautious. He waved the others to a halt, then motioned for Marty to follow.

"What about me?" Zach asked.

"You stay with the others for now," Caulie instructed. "I'm not goin' any further till I know the lay of the land."

Without pausing any longer, Caulie nudged his horse into a slow trot and drew out his pistol. He crossed the low ridge which separated Marty's place from the Mexican farms in Ox Hollow. Down below two of the farmhouses blazed brightly. The remaining houses spit fire from their front windows at a dozen or so encircling riflemen.

"We could ride 'em down, Caulie, but they'd likely shoot some of us to pieces," Marty said, scratching the stubble of his beard. "If we closed in on 'em from cover, we'd have a dandy crossfire goin' for us."

"Take Dix and the men from town," Caulie said, examining the terrain carefully. "Use the cornfield as cover. See if you can't catch 'em off guard. I'll lead the others around to the south. That way we can squeeze 'em to the middle."

"They could turn on you, Caulie. You'll only have Marsh and those boys with you."

"I don't figure 'em to run my way, Marty. If they do, we'll take our toll."

"You can't shoot 'em all, Caulie. I'll have Dix go with you. And unless Marsh has lost his eye, he used to be a fair shot with a rifle."

"Sure. Now let's get to it."

They returned and divided the small band. Caulie then led Dix, Marsh, and the boys off across the ridge and then back toward the encircled cabins. Caulie dismounted and asked his companions to leave their mounts in a small ravine. Soon thereafter Caulie spied the first of several dark-shirted marksmen. Each wore a flour sack over his head, but even so, Caulie made out the strutting figure of Matt Simpson in the center.

"Give it up, you fools!" young Simpson shouted. "We've got more coal oil. Won't be long before the rest of you are fryin' like your cousins down the hollow."

"We go nowhere!" the powerful voice of Hernando Salazar replied. "What right do you have to shoot our cows, burn our homes?"

"This right!" Simpson declared, waving for his men to resume firing. The front of Hernando's house absorbed two dozen rapid shots. Pieces of door splintered. The little glass remaining in the windows shattered into fragments. A woman cried, and a child shrieked in terror.

That's enough of that, Caulie told himself as he edged closer. He could feel Zach's nervous breathing as the boy crawled alongside.

"Wait for me to fire, then shoot," Caulie whispered as he made his way to a pile of boulders on the edge of a field. It was the last cover available, and it offered a perfect shield from which to open up on Simpson's raiders.

"Pa, I never shot at a man before," Zach mumbled. Caulie steadied the boy's hands on the rifle, then patted Zach's shoulder.

"No real need to think much about it, son. Just shoot in that direction. We're not here so much to kill as to pry 'em loose from their perch."

Caulie swallowed. It was a lie, and Zach's eyes knew it. Caulfield Blake hadn't ridden seven miles to chase bushwhackers. He'd come to kill Simpson men, come to make war on young Matt and the Jenkinses and all others who meant to do Hannah harm.

"We're ready," Dix called from behind the far end of the rocks.

"Then it's time," Caulie said, leveling his rifle at the closest of the hooded killers and easing back the trigger. The Winchester spouted flame, and the gunman whirled around and collapsed.

"Matt, they're behind us!" a second rifleman called seconds before Dix's bullet shattered a thigh. "Lord, help us!"

Young Simpson shouted to the others and started toward the cornfield. Rifles from the house killed a third man, and a fourth went down shortly. Matt's companions were in a wild panic as they raced toward the safety of the cornfield. At that moment Marty's men aimed and fired a deadly volley at the oncoming riders. Two more fell, and another clutched a shoulder.

"What now, Pa?" Zach asked as the confused raiders rushed in a dozen directions.

"You watch yourself," Caulie said, pushing Zach's head back behind the shelter of the boulder. "Fire only if they come by."

By now the survivors had reached their horses. Marty's group continued to fire from the cornfield, and the Mexicans at the farmhouses had rushed out to finish off one lame gunman who'd headed that way. Matt Simpson tossed aside his hood and kicked his horse into a gallop. The Jenkins brothers trailed along behind, and a pair of young cowboys raced to catch up.

"I know that's you over there, Blake!" Matt shouted, pointing directly toward the boulders. "You won't find me as easy to ambush as my father!"

Caulie aimed and fired, but young Simpson moved away. His Winchester struck the young man's horse in the ribs, and the horse rose high into the air. Marsh and Carter fired, too, and one of them hit the horse a second time. The animal whined in pain, then fell on one shoulder.

"Abe!" Matt yelled.

Abe Jenkins raced by, and Matt Simpson crawled up behind the veteran gunman with a quickness Caulie had rarely seen from a white man. The remaining raiders then headed away, pausing only long enough to set the cornfield on fire.

"Dix, see if you can get that fire stamped out," Caulie said before rushing toward the farmhouse. "I'll see who's hurt."

"Marsh, boys, come along!" Dix cried. "That fire'll take half the county if it's not put out quick."

Marty already had his crew busy beating down the flames, and Hernando's youngsters were out there as well. Caulie let them deal with the fire. His eyes were watching Hernando.

"I thank you for your gift," Hernando said as he sank, exhausted, to his knees. "If you had not come . . ."

"Wasn't just me," Caulie explained. "Was Marty saw 'em come. We had lots of help. We didn't altogether kill off those skunks, but we stung 'em a bit."

"Yes, and they hurt us, too," Hernando said, motioning toward the flames that even now consumed half the little settlement. "They killed Jesus Cortes and his wife. Their little Anita, too. My own boy Carlos is shot. The Rojas family will go now. The Vargases as well. Only Roberto and I will remain, and for how long? Who will die next?"

"You, me, Simpson. Maybe next time they'll surprise us."

"But there will be a next time, won't there, amigo?"

"Seems like there always is."

"When our fathers were alive, we would have gone down to Senor Simpson and set him ablaze. Ay, we would have killed him like a mad bull. Even the wolf does not hunt his own kind."

"No, that's left for men. And old man Simpson, well, he's got an appetite for land. Our mistake was lettin' him settle here in the first place. Pa thought him to have a bad eye, and he said as much, but you know how softhearted Emma Siler was. Ernest was dead, and I'll admit Simpson offered a fair price for the land. Now we're payin'."

"You went away once. You came back. Is it so hard to leave the place of your birth?"

"Hard enough."

"Maybe we should all go. There has been already too much bleeding."

"Maybe," Caulie agreed. "I've read death in Simpson's eyes. And I've never read such greed and hate on one man's face. There'll be more dyin'."

"Yes. Next time he will come by night."

Caulie nodded, then turned away. He headed toward the

cornfield, but by then the fire was under control. A line of weary people passed buckets from a well to a pair of men who slung water on the fringe of the smoldering cornfield. Marty and Dix had the others slapping wet canvas against the opposite edge of the fire.

"Anybody dead?" Dix asked as Caulie approached.

"The Cortes family. I think they caught the first charge. Hernando's got a boy hurt. Most of 'em are headin' out."

"Can hardly blame 'em. Even in a good year the corn crop barely pays the bills."

"I just hate to see the land go to Simpson."

"I think that's goin' to be the least of our worries, Caulie. After today, it's bound to be all-out war. You ready for that?"

"I'll have to be. 'Cause Hannah won't be leavin'."

"The boys did just fine today," Dix observed. "Zach was a little shaky, but that Carter squared up just fine, kept up a steady fire you'd been glad to've seen at Johnsonville."

"That's good. Before we're through, there'll be need of such talents," Caulie said.

"Like as not before Simpson's finished, I'll have Charlie firin' a Winchester."

"Maybe Hernando's right, Dix."

"Oh?"

"He says our fathers would've ridden right out there and burned old man Simpson out."

"They might've tried," Dix admitted. "That's Simpson's game, though."

"Dix, we've fought Comanches and chased Yank cavalry across half the South. We can deal with Henry Simpson, and we will."

Chapter Nine

Hannah sat on the porch and mended a pair of Zach's trousers. Whenever she was most nervous, she took to sewing. Usually the work took her mind off her troubles, but all she managed to do this time was prick her fingers and miss stitches.

"Ma, you hurt yourself," little Sally remarked as she sat down and leaned her small head against her mother's side.

"It's nothing, Honeybee," Hannah told the child. "Where have your brothers gotten off to? I haven't seen them the past hour."

"They rode off," Sally said, pointing to the south.

"Not those two," Hannah said, smiling as Sally squirmed and giggled. "Wylie and Todd."

"They're back at the pond splashing around, Ma."

"Why don't you go fetch them, child. We might have a little lunch, don't you think?"

"They don't like me to watch them swim, Ma. Todd threw mud at me one time."

"They know better than to go in the water without anybody back there to watch them. Now go fetch them, Honeybee. Tell them I said to come up quickly."

"Yes'm."

Sally scampered off, and Hannah set aside her sewing. Her fingers lacked the touch today, and when she gazed again toward the south, she couldn't help seeing the pillar of smoke rising from the distance. Something was burning, most likely the hovels over at Ox Hollow or Marty Cabot's place.

"I never should have let the boys go," she grumbled. "That's why Caulie came back, so they would be safe from all this."

A vision of Zach slung across a saddle filtered into her mind, and she gasped. Instantly she shook off the thought. After all, Caulie would look out for them. Marsh was there as well. They'd never let her children come into any real danger.

"Ma, I told them," Sally said, reappearing at her mother's side. "They've been fishing. Didn't catch so much as a worm, though."

"Well, come along and help me ready lunch. Maybe your father will be home in time to join us."

"I'll set the table for everybody, then. You think Uncle Dix will come? I wish he'd bring Katie. She gave me a bonnet, remember?"

"Yes, dear," Hannah said, smiling as she marveled at the simple way five-year-olds looked at life. Hannah wished she could think of bonnets or anything save the distant smoke marking the scene where her loved ones were riding into terrible peril.

Midday came and went, but without a glimpse of Marsh and the boys. Hannah resumed her sewing, taking time out only to see that little Todd and Wylie had their early afternoon rest. Given to their own inclinations, the four-year-olds would run till they dropped.

By two o'clock the twins had napped long enough. They were chasing their sister around the house when Hannah hollered for them to hush.

"I hear something!" she yelled. "Get on over here, children."

Sally tugged her reluctant brothers toward their mother, and the four of them sat together for a moment. Hannah reached into her sewing basket and fingered the revolver. Down below, near the creek, horses were splashing their way through the sodden bank. She counted two, three, maybe more animals. She held her breath and prayed it would be Marsh. She fought off darker thoughts—visions of Matt Simpson's arrogant face bringing home the dead.

"Hannah, we're back!" Marsh finally bellowed. At the sound of their father's voice, the children instantly darted out the door. By the time Marsh Merritt emerged on horseback from a stand of oaks, he was surrounded by grinning faces and eager arms.

"Marsh?" Hannah called as he halted long enough to pull the boys up on the horse behind him. Sally crawled onto her father's lap. Still there wasn't a hint of anyone else. Then Carter rode past his father, his straw-colored hair and pale face blackened with smoke from the burning cornfield. Zach joined them shortly, his normally bright eyes clouded with shock and fatigue.

Hannah walked out to greet them. As she held the bay's bridle, Zach managed a faint grin.

"Is everyone . . . did anyone come to harm?" she asked.

"One of the Mexican families got themselves killed," Zach explained. "Happened before we got there. Carlos Salazar was shot, too. You remember Carlos, Ma. He brought that spotted pony over last winter, the one Sally likes to ride."

"And the others?" Hannah asked, turning to Marsh. "They're all right?"

"Simpson lost some hands," Marsh explained. "But Dix and Marty came through fine."

"Caulie?" she asked nervously.

"Oh, he's just fine, Ma," Zach said, brightening at the mention of his father's name. "Should've seen him, Ma. He was just like a general, shoutin' commands, cuttin' those Simpson riders to pieces."

"I thought maybe you'd bring him back with you," Hannah said as Zach rolled off his horse and leaned against her. "He's out at Dix's place all by himself, and . . ."

"He knows he doesn't belong here," Carter declared. "Not anymore. I made it pretty clear to him."

"You what?" Hannah asked. "Carter Merritt! It was I asked him here. He's more than welcome if he chooses to come, and I'll not hear you speak ill of him."

"He ran out on us, Ma. You forget that? How do we know he won't do it again?"

"He won't," Zach argued. "He kept lookin' back to make sure I was all right. He cares, Ma. About you, too."

Marsh had sat silently for a time. Now he helped the little ones down, then instructed Carter to fetch the horses along to the barn.

"Sally, Todd, Wylie, you help your brother. Take my horse, Todd. Wylie, you take the bay. Zach's pretty well spent, what with his midnight antics and this business today. It's best we get him along to the house."

"Sure, Pa," the little ones said as one. Carter then climbed down, took his horse in tow, and waved the little ones along.

"You angry with me, Marsh?" Zach asked when the others had passed from view. "You always say a man ought to tend his own animal."

"Won't hurt the little ones to lend a hand, and Carter knows what to do. I'm in need of a rest just now, and you look to be the same."

"Come on, scamp," Hannah said, leading the sweaty thirteen-year-old toward the house. "I'll see if we can't fill a tub. You look to need a good scrubbing."

"Yes'm," Zach admitted. "I feel like I've been cooked on a spit and am ready for the smokehouse."

"Smell like it, too," Marsh declared.

Hannah laughed, then left Marsh to help Zach drag out the washtub while she set kettles of water on the stove. By the time the water was hot, Carter had the horses in their stalls. The tub was soon full, and Zach soaked in it like there was no tomorrow.

"Never will get me to fight in a battle," Todd commented as he brought his brother a cake of soap. "Not if you have to take a bath midweek 'cause of it."

Hannah laughed as she shooed the little ones along. There

were afternoon chores waiting, and all sorts of debris was clogging Carpenter Creek following the flood. Marsh soon had Carter hacking away at tangles of willow limbs and cottonwood saplings. The little ones strained to carry buckets of water from the well to the near-empty water barrels. Sally fed the hogs and watched her little brothers. Hannah settled in beside the tub and rubbed Zach's weary shoulders. It had been a good while since they'd had a serious talk, and she could read the need in Zach's bloodshot eyes.

"I asked him to come home last night," Zach told her. "He is welcome, isn't he?"

"Always has been. He was born here, and he mostly built this house."

"Ma, I know you told me before, but I've got to ask. How come he left? I mean, I see how much he misses you. It's on his face. How come a man who feels so strongly would go away? Doesn't make sense."

"I know," she said, stroking his stringy hair. "I used to think it was because he'd outgrown us, changed so that he didn't belong. Each year I'm a little less sure."

"Carter doesn't much like him. Marsh, neither."

"Carter felt it more than you, I suppose. All of a sudden he was the man of the family. Marsh lifted that burden. As for Marsh, it's natural he should feel strongly, especially with you taking to Caulie like you have."

"He's my pa."

"It's more than that," she said, splashing water onto the boy's face. "You're so much like him, Zach. When he was little, Caulie Blake could ride the wind. I never saw a boy who could fill the day with more mischief. Unless maybe it was you."

"Oh, Ma."

"So don't blame Marsh if he acts like Caulie's a bit of a thief. He is, you know. He's stolen your heart. Deep down Marsh knows there's a rightness in that, and he doesn't hold it against you, Zach. Be patient. It's going to take us all a bit of time to figure out our feelings."

"I was considerin' goin' over to the cabin, maybe stayin' there tonight. He's all alone there, Ma. And if I . . ."

"No, Zach. Your place is here."

"And Pa's?"

"Is where he feels he belongs. If he wants, he'll come here. Caulie never in his life did something he didn't choose to do. It's cost him a lot, that headstrong way of his. But it's made him strong, too."

"You still love him, don't you?"

"He's part of me, Zach, just like you and your brothers and sister. We grew up together. A lot of my life passed in the company of Caulfield Blake. But now I feel we're partly strangers. Seven years is a long time."

"I know. I feel it, too."

"And I'm not altogether certain I can forgive him, Zach. The hurt is deep."

"Yeah, but he came when you asked."

Hannah nodded, then left to fetch a towel. When she returned, Zach took the towel, wrapped it around his waist, and shivered his way to the side room he shared with Carter and the twins. Hannah marveled at how small and vulnerable he appeared. And she wondered how she could have been persuaded to allow little Zach to ride off to Ox Hollow.

She heated the tub twice more that afternoon. First Marsh and Carter washed away their weariness. Then the little ones scrubbed away creek mud and horse sweat. After frying a chicken for supper, she led Marsh out toward the creek to watch the sunset.

"It's been a time since we did this," he told her. "What brought you to bring me here?"

"I don't know," Hannah told him. "I guess I just needed to hold on to someone's hand just now."

"I remember the first time we walked here. You called me Caulie."

"We came here often, especially when Pa's cabin stood just the other side of the creek from Caulie's place."

"You've been thinking a lot about him lately."

"I know. Forgive me?"

"Nothing to forgive, Hannah. Only thing is, I'm beginning to wonder just where I fit in. Zach's slipped away already, and I see you drifting, too. You're my wife, Hannah. Your name's Merritt now."

"Have I ever given you reason to think I've lost sight of that?"

"No, and I'd keep it that way. I don't want him here, Hannah. It's one thing that you didn't trust me to handle Henry Simpson. Now I've lost a son, too. I won't have Caulfield Blake in my house. People in town are already talking."

"People in town," Hannah said in disgust. "They've been the problem more than once, them and their talk. Can you forget who built that house? It's his home more than anybody's."

"That was long ago, Hannah. It's my sweat that's kept the ranch going, not Caulfield Blake's reputation. He wouldn't try to take the title back, would he?"

"Henry Simpson maybe. Not Caulie."

"You'd invite him to stay, though. Do your feelings run so deep that I ought to reconsider my place?"

"Of course not," she said, intertwining her arm with Marsh's. "You're my husband. I've got no other. I worry about him, though."

"I thought him equal to each and every task," Marsh couldn't help saying. "The way Zach talks, Caulfield Blake built the mountains and dug the riverbeds."

"He acts that way sometimes, Marsh, but it's all bluff and bluster. He hurts. And I can't help wondering if he hasn't come back to die."

"Die?"

"It's one way to come home, Marsh. He never took chances when he fought Comanches. He knew we depended on him. It seems to me he's taken grave risks since getting here."

"You think he'd take less chances if you were still married?"

"Don't you?"

"Yes," Marsh admitted.

"Caulie's not so different. He puts on a poker face, but he cares as much as anybody."

"More's the pity."

"I know," she said sadly. "I know."

Chapter Ten

Caulfield Blake stayed at Ox Hollow long enough to see the dead laid to rest. Roberto Salazar carved the names of the slain on planks saved from the ruin of the Cortes barn. By dusk the ashes of the houses had cooled, and wagons laden with sullen farmers and their families rolled down the road toward town and a new future farther west.

"This shouldn't go unpunished," Dix Stewart declared. "We all saw Matt Simpson here. I'll have a warrant sworn out. Justice will be done."

"You really think anybody's goin' to serve that warrant?" Marty asked. "Who's goin' to hang Henry Simpson's grandson? The boy's just seventeen. Besides, no one's forgotten what happened to Caulie after Austin was strung up."

"I'm goin' to the sheriff," Dix said. "I can't believe the law's totally disappeared from Texas."

"Whose law?" Caulie asked. "The same law that kept young Perry from gettin' his papers filed?"

"I'll swear out the warrant," Dix argued. "Will somebody else bear witness?"

"I will," Joe Stovall said. "I saw the Simpson boy and Abe Jenkins besides. Don't know that it'll do a lick of good, but I'll put my name to the paper, Dix."

"Me, too," Art Powell added. "We stuck together across half of Tennessee. I can't see goin' separate ways now."

"Marty?" Dix asked.

"I've got my family to look to."

"Caulie?"

"It's a long way back to the cabin, Dix."

"Then stay the night with us in town. Rita's not lost her touch with a skillet. I can't believe you'd choose jerked beef over chicken and dumplin's."

"All right," Caulie said, sighing. "But it's like as not to stir up worse trouble."

"Worse?" Joe asked. "There's been murder done here today. How can it get worse?"

Caulie stared grimly toward the Simpson place. They all knew it could get worse. And most suspected it would.

Caulie found himself and Dix Stewart received coldly in town.

"What's that you say?" the sheriff asked when Dix related the morning massacre. "You did what? Killed raiders at Ox Hollow! Simpson men, you say? And Mexicans were killed as well. I never heard of the like. Why didn't you send for me straightaway?"

"Would you have come?" Caulie asked.

"It's my duty to settle disputes. Now there's been bloodshed on both sides. It's apt to get out of hand. Now you tell me Matt Simpson led these raiders. Matt's just a boy. He's a trifle wild, I'll grant, but he wouldn't go shooting up farmers without a reason. Those Mexicans, the Salazars in particular, are always stirring up folks. If things are so unfair, let 'em go back to Mexico."

"Their grandfather fought with Sam Houston at San Jacinto," Dix raged. "Their people have lived in Texas two hundred years."

"So they claim. I wouldn't put a lot of stock in such talk, though," the sheriff said, laying loudly. "It's easy to claim you're this and that."

"You mean like callin' yourself a colonel?" Caulie asked.

"You watch your talk, Blake. I barely kept Matt from pullin' on you th'other day at the hotel. You keep insultin' Henry Simpson, you might find riders comin' to pay *you* a call."

"Then when Dix brought me into town, you'd likely call me a troublemaker, too, huh?" Caulie asked. "I'm warnin' you, Sheriff. People won't stand by and watch night riders terrorize their neighbors."

"Oh? Why don't you go back to your horses up on the Clear Fork, Blake? Leave me to handle things hereabouts."

Caulie started to reply, but Dix turned him toward the door.

"You were right," Dix whispered. "There is no law in Simpson. We'll wind up settlin' things ourselves."

Caulfield Blake couldn't complain about coming to town, though. Rita had a true talent in the kitchen, and sitting down to supper at a real table, surrounded by friends, took him back to other, gentler times. But even as he helped little Charlie Stewart clear the supper dishes, Caulie couldn't help thinking that such peaceful interludes rarely lasted long. And whenever he felt safe, secure, the dark storm clouds of war gathered, and he wound up facing the stiffest trials of all.

It was a sobering thought, and Caulie was tempted to ride back to the cabin that night.

"You can't go yet," Charlie pleaded. "Pa said you can have my bed tonight. I can sleep in a blanket roll, just like a real range cowboy. Tomorrow Ma's goin' to pack us a picnic basket. We can go down to the pond and have a time of it. Besides, you're supposed to tell me about chasing mustangs up on the Clear Fork."

"I never promised to do that," Caulie grumbled.

"Well, no, but Katie said you would. You used to tell her

stories, or so she says. You ought to do the same for me. I'm half named for you, remember?"

Caulie grinned as the boy stared up with wistful eyes.

"Named for me, you say?" Caulie asked, forcing a stern look to his face.

"Charles Blake Stewart. That's me. The Blake's you, right?"

"Well, I'm not the only Blake to've crossed this range."

"But you're the one that Pa rode with in the war. Katie told me all about how you saved his life up in Tennessee. You're Zach Merritt's pa, too. Zach and I go fishing sometimes."

"Well, I guess I'm good for a story," Caulie said, surrendering. "After all, it's late to ride east."

"None too safe, either. Men've been waylaid on that road, especially if they tangle with Matt Simpson."

"And what would you know about that?" Caulie asked.

"People talk," Charlie said with fiery eyes. "I listen."

Charlie suddenly seemed much older than his ten years and slender shoulders suggested. Later on, as Caulie spun tales of the buffalo range, of Fort Griffin and The Flat, he felt the boy's hand on a shoulder that had felt no such closeness for half a decade. Caulie shuddered, and Charlie crept closer.

"It's time we got to our beds now," Caulie announced as he wrapped up the tale. "Wouldn't want to miss that picnic tomorrow."

"No, sir," Charlie agreed. "Ma plans to fry a chicken."

Caulie grinned, then left the room as Charlie began shedding clothes.

"Looks as if you've made a friend," Rita observed as she met Caulie in the hall. "Does him good. Town's no place to raise a boy."

"Why don't you go back to the ranch, then?"

"Maybe we will when this Simpson business is over. Things being what they are, I wouldn't feel safe."

"It's bound to get worse, Rita."

"Yes, but now you're here. I feel better knowing Dix has someone to depend on."

"There are others."

"But no one to lead. It hasn't proven healthy to be a leader in this town, Caulie. Those who've tried haven't lived to count their grandchildren."

"I feel like I'm bringing a storm down on you all. I had Zach out there with me today. Rita, he's not much older than Charlie there. What is it that hurries men to their deaths?"

"That's easy," she said grimly. "Henry Simpson."

Caulie nodded sadly, then walked back down the hall and quietly slipped out of his clothes.

"Uncle Caulie?" Charlie asked as Caulie burrowed his way into the soft feather mattress.

"Charlie?"

"Good night. I'm glad you came back."

"Night, son," Caulie said, wishing to high heaven he could say that to Carter or Zach. But it was sometimes too late to mend a fence. The stock had escaped, and most wild things never really take to a halter.

Caulie slept peacefully well into the next morning. By the time he opened his eyes, Rita had exchanged his shirt for a fresh one from the store, and Charlie had put a shine to the battered boots and brushed the dust from Caulie's weather-beaten hat.

"I believe I've fallen into good company," Caulie remarked with a smile as Rita poured him a cup of steaming coffee. "And now I hear we're to have a picnic."

"Well, in truth Katherine said we need a holiday. She's been planning the outing for a month. She's got her eye on young John Moffitt down at the livery. I suspect he's to come along. It will do us all some good, though. Town's not so pleasant a place to be as it once was."

"Has Matt Simpson been by?"

"No, but I suspect he's heard about Dix's visit to the sheriff. Simpson has his spies everywhere."

"Maybe we should stay close to the store today."

"Nonsense. We'll only be down at Oak Grove."

"Oak Grove?" Caulie asked, his hands trembling slightly.

"As I recall, you've cause to remember the place. Wasn't that where you asked Hannah to . . ."

"Yes," he said, cutting her off.

"Sorry, Caulie. I didn't intend to open up old wounds. Maybe we should choose another spot."

"It's a good place. Simpson hasn't pried it away from Hannah?"

"She has a memory, too, Caulie. She sold off most of those southern sections, but she held on to the grove south of the market road, the pond, and the pastureland up to Marty's place."

"Good for her."

"Good for you, too. That stretch was part of Simpson's price for opening up his dam, you know. Now he's lost his bargaining strength."

"So he'll try to take it instead."

"Probably."

But Henry Simpson had yet to stamp the Diamond S brand on the grove, and that afternoon Caulie, young Moffitt, and the Stewart clan enjoyed a brief diversion. After gorging themselves on fried chicken and sweet corn, Katie and her beau wandered off in the wood. Dix and Rita packed up the leftover food, then took a stroll.

"Guess it's just you and me, huh, Charlie?" Caulie asked.

"Oh, they do this all the time," the boy said. "That's why I bring along some fishing line."

"Enough for two?"

"Sure," Charlie said, grinning widely as he pulled two balls of line from a pocket. "Come on. I know the place where the catfish love to hide."

As Caulie shed his shoes and followed Charlie out onto a fallen oak trunk, he felt as if he'd slipped back twenty years. He and Dix had fished that pond more than once.

"Swimming's fair here, too, though the water's still a little cool," Charlie explained.

"Water's deep."

"Cats like it that way in the summer. Pa says it tickles their whiskers."

Caulie laughed, and Charlie cried out with excitement as his line strained under the weight of a fish.

"You've got one," Caulie said, watching intently as Charlie played the catfish, then began pulling him in bit by bit.

"Ma fries cats just about as fine as she fries chicken," Charlie declared as he drew the fish into the shallows before flipping it onto the bank. "He's a big 'un."

"Sure is," Caulie agreed. "Think he's got some cousins down there?"

"More'n a few," the boy said as he ran a string through the fish's gills and tied one end to a small oak sapling. He then returned the secured fish to the water.

They fished for close to an hour before they accumulated four fish. Charlie announced that was enough, flung off his shirt, shed his trousers, and splashed into the pond. The sight of the boy swimming away the afternoon heat was more than Caulie could bear. In an instant he was out of his clothes and in the water as well.

"Race you to that stump!" Charlie challenged, and the dash was on. Caulie closed to within a foot of the blond-haired demon, then eased off so Charlie could win.

"Ah, you gave up," Charlie complained. "Pa does it, too."

"Give up?" Caulie complained. "Wore me out, you tadpole."

Charlie grinned, then hauled himself atop the stump and jumped into the pond. Moments later the boy was shoveling water at Caulie's face. Caulie took a deep breath and lunged forward, capturing Charlie and securely holding the boy in place.

"Am I under arrest, marshal?" Charlie asked.

"Yes, sir, you are," Caulie said, dragging the boy through the shallows and tossing him onto the bank.

"You're a pretty fair swimmer for an old man," Charlie remarked as he sprawled out in the soft grass.

"Remind me not to wrestle any more worms," Caulie said. "It's too exhausting."

"Fun, though."

Caulie couldn't help laughing. His grin soon faded as he spied a line of hooded riders cutting across the pasture from the southwest. Instantly Caulie dragged Charlie Stewart behind cover, and the two scrambled into their clothes.

"It's some of Simpson's men," Charlie declared. "They come to town sometimes that way when they don't want anybody to see who it is."

"They bother your pa?"

"Once. They ran off some Mexicans. Nobody said it was Matt Simpson, but everybody knows."

"Sure," Caulie said, pulling on his boots and buttoning up his shirt.

"You going after 'em, Uncle Caulie?"

"I expect so."

"Be careful," the boy said, clinging to Caulie's arm as a smaller Carter had the morning of the hanging. "They shoot people real dead. I've seen it."

"So have I," Caulie said, gently pulling away from the youngster. "Don't fret. I've faced 'em before."

"Pa'll be going with you, won't he?"

"Maybe."

Charlie gazed down at his bare feet, and Caulie searched for words of comfort. He knew none. Instead he lifted the boy up, slung him over one shoulder, and carried him the fifty yards to where Rita had left the wagon. By that time John Moffitt and Katie were back. Dix and Rita joined them shortly.

"See if you can help this cowboy get his boots on, Kate," Caulie said as he checked the cylinder on his pistol.

"There are too many of them," she answered. "Pa?"

"I'm goin', too," John announced. "I can shoot a rifle."

Caulie glanced at Dix, who nodded.

"You get along back to town," Dix told Rita. "Bolt the door, too. They could be headed that way. Give the Simpson place a wide berth. I'll be home when I can get there."

"Me, too," John said, gripping Kate's hand before turning away.

"Leave John your horse, Charlie," Dix said, helping his son into the bed of the wagon. "Caulie?"

"Sure," Caulie answered, slipping his Winchester out of its saddle scabbard and passing the rifle along to young Moffitt. "Let's go."

The three riders charged off toward the road, but Caulie soon waved his companions to a halt. Smoke rose from the south, and the three riders turned toward Ox Hollow. All along the way Caulie envisioned a scene of death and destruction. But none of his nightmare thoughts prepared him for the cruel reality he discovered.

The cabins remained as before. The smoke came from a blazing cow barn. Out front the remaining farmers huddled with their children around a single white oak. From a branch hung a long gray object. Riding closer, Caulie saw it was the body of Hernando Salazar.

"They came again," fourteen-year-old Carlos cried out as Caulie slid down from his horse. "Uncle Roberto was away in the fields. My arm is no good. What could Papa do? They shot him. They they do this! I will kill them all!"

"Could you see any of their faces?" Dix asked.

"They were covered," Carlos answered, "but we know who it was. I have heard the laugh of Matthew Simpson often. He will choke on that laughter."

"For God's sake cut him down," Caulie said, turning his face away from the spinning body of his old friend. "I swear there'll be payment for this."

"It's no use," Roberto said, cradling his brother's body as John Moffitt cut the ropes. "They will come again and again. We shoot six of them, and ten return to kill my brother."

"You can't give up," Dix cried. "It's Simpson who's behind this, and we'll have to settle accounts."

"You settle with him," Roberto said angrily. "I have a brother to bury and children to protect. There's been enough blood shed over this place."

Carlos gazed sorrowfully at his uncle, and Roberto set Hernando's body down, then led the boy away.

"We're not needed here," Caulie announced to his companions. "It's best we ride on."

Dix nodded, and John Moffitt climbed back atop his horse. The three of them turned and rode toward the Cabot ranch.

Chapter Eleven

The question which flooded Caulfield Blake's mind was where Simpson's hooded riders would strike next. He was tempted to return to town with Dix Stewart, but it seemed unlikely even Simpson would so openly defy the sheriff as to raid Dix's store. Marty, on the other hand, was isolated. And Hannah . . . well, Simpson's whole ranch lay between the Bar Double B and help.

"What good can you do up at that cabin, all alone as you'll be?" Dix asked as Caulie turned his horse northward.

"I'll be at hand should riders head up Carpenter Creek. The stream's too swollen to be crossed just anywhere at present. Anyone hitting Hannah's place will have to come by way of the cabin or else slosh through half of Siler's Hollow."

"And if Simpson decides to hit the cabin itself?"

"I'll be ready," Caulie said, his eyes flashing with a fire brought on by the memory of Hernando's dangling corpse. "Get some of that dynamite ready, Dix. We might just have a surprise in store for Mr. Simpson."

Dix frowned at the notion of raiding the Diamond S, but he nodded his understanding.

* * *

As night fell, Caulie dozed lightly on the floor of the cabin. Two loaded Winchesters stood at arm's length. His dreams filled with recollections of death, of friends swept away by musket fire during the war, of a father slain by Comanche arrows. He awoke a little after midnight to the sound of flapping wings. A great horned owl had swept down onto the porch to snatch a small rabbit in its claws.

"What's this?" Caulie called.

The owl peered toward the cabin, its eerie eyes probing the darkness like two foreboding circles. It uttered a chilling cry, and Caulie recalled how Indians deemed an owl's call a poor omen.

"Go away, owl," he told the bird. "You've saddled me with enough bad luck for twenty men. Go haunt someone else."

The owl sank its claws into the rabbit until the life flowed out of the little ball of fur. Then the great bird flapped off into the trees.

"You're not the only one to hunt by night," Caulie whispered. "I've done my share of stalkin' and killin' in the darkness." He knew there would be more yet to come. Henry Simpson wanted stopping, and the night was always the ally of the weaker force.

Darkness was also a perfect shield. Its mists cast spells, or so it seemed to Caulfield Blake. Down by the Colorado a world of shadows, real or imagined, haunted the river. Many a time he'd spun tales of ghosts and Comanche spirits that terrified the boys. They often seemed all too true.

Caulie remembered those stories as he drifted off. Death and despair seemed to smother the air. And when a horse raced up the hill, Caulie rose instantly and huddled beside the front window with one of the Winchesters.

"Who's out there?" he called.

"Mr. Blake?" a shaky voice answered.

"I know who I am," Caulie replied angrily. "Who'd you be?"

"It's Caleb, Mr. Blake. Caleb Cabot. My pa sent me . . . sent me to fetch you. We've got trouble, Mr. Blake."

Caulie cradled the rifle in his hands as he crawled around to the door. It was hard to see anyone or anything in the shrouded night. Fog hung heavily across the hillside. Finally Caulie located a small boy close to Charlie Stewart's size and age.

"You Marty's boy?" Caulie asked as he blinked the sleep from his eyes.

"Yes, sir," the youngster said, trembling. "We've got trouble. Get your horse and follow me."

"What sort of trouble?" Caulie asked, reading the concern in the boy's eyes. "What's happened?"

"Nothin' just yet. Leastwise not when I started out. Some riders came. Pa saw 'em. Me, I'd never noticed, but Pa's got eyes like a hawk. He said to tell you the Jenkins boys were there with Matt Simpson. Some others, too."

Caulie nodded grimly. Well, at least he knew where they were. By now they were likely shooting bullets and setting Marty's house alight.

"I'll get my horse," Caulie said, stepping into his boots and grabbing a shirt.

"You get dressed. I'll saddle your horse," Caleb said. "Just hurry. When I left, the little ones were awful scared."

Caulie couldn't help sighing. Little ones? Caleb was hardly four feet five, and he was worried about little ones? Caulie threw on his clothes, buckled on his gun belt, and set off for the barn. True to his word, young Caleb had the big black saddled and ready to ride.

"Son, there's no point to you comin' along," Caulie said as he climbed atop the horse.

"That's my family back there," Caleb explained.

"And you'll do 'em a whole lot of good, won't you? You've got no gun. You fetched me. Let me tend to that. You know the Bar Double B?"

"Sure," Caleb said, nodding.

"Ride out there and tell the folks there what you just told me. Have 'em stay put, though. You, too. I'll bring your family out once it's over."

"I don't know, Mr. Blake. Pa said I was to bring you . . ."

"You did a whale of a job of it, too, son. I know you're worried, but trust me to know what's best. Ride along to the Bar Double B. Wait for us there. Won't be so long as it'll feel."

Caleb nodded and turned his horse northward. Caulie rode south, toward Marty and what was probably by now a desperate fight for survival.

Caulie slapped his horse into a gallop and raced along the darkened ridge toward the Cabot place. Mesquite thorns tore at his arms and face. Rocks slowed the horse. But the surefooted stallion continued. The horse seemed to sense the urgency in its rider's shallow breaths. Caulie crossed the treacherous three miles in half an hour.

By that time Marty's barn lit half the county. The livestock whined anxiously as they fled in every direction. Marty returned the attackers' gunfire from the house. A second rifle flashed from one of the rear bedrooms.

"Give it up, Cabot!" Abe Jenkins bellowed. "We'll burn the house next. All we want is you. Come out, and we'll let the young ones go."

"Hang yourself!" Marty replied, firing a shot that nearly took Abe's ear off.

"Suit yourself!" Matt Simpson said as he waved his men forward. Two raced toward the house just ahead of Caulie. They were outlined by the flaming barn, and Caulie aimed and fired in a single motion. Both fell in turn, and Abe turned his attention toward the approaching horseman. Caulie raced for the house, then jumped off his horse and ran to the door. Bullets followed his shadow.

"You fool," Marty said as Caulie slid inside. "That's a mighty fine way to get yourself killed. Where's Caleb?"

"I sent him along to Hannah."

"That'll be a comfort to his ma. I've got Court back in the kitchen with a rifle. I sent Eve and the little ones down to the root cellar."

"Fine idea so long as the Jenkins boys don't burn the house down atop 'em."

"Well, I guess it's up to us to see that doesn't happen."

"Your barn's gone."

"I've built more barns'n I can remember, Caulie. Don't you worry yourself over that."

"I feel responsible."

"You're not. Old man Simpson's had his eye on my place for years. Tried to run me off this winter. Kept me from gettin' horses to market. We made out, though."

"We will this time, too."

"Hope you're right. They've got us trapped real sweet here. I never liked fightin' in buildings, Caulie. I'd rather be out there in the open, with the dark on my side."

"There's precious little dark. The barn's seen to that. Those boys have to know the better part of the county's seen the fire. Others'll come along soon. Their time's about gone."

The raiders thought so, too. A second pair raced toward the house. Caulie sent one rushing backward, and Marty killed the other with a clean shot through the lungs.

"You comin' out, Cabot?" Abe asked.

"Why don't you come along in like your friends, Abe," Marty answered. "Let's see how brave you are."

Abe showed no inclination to rush the house, and his companions shared his caution. The rifle fire resumed, but most of it was poorly directed. Suddenly three rifles opened up on the kitchen from short range. Glass shattered, and Marty raced toward the back of the house. As he reached the kitchen door, it flew open, and a dark-hooded stranger stepped into view holding a pistol to the head of young Court Cabot.

"Pa!" Court cried as the killer turned the pistol toward Marty.

Caulie whirled and fired. His bullet shattered the gunman's jaw and tore through the brain. The raider collapsed like a rag doll, and Court scrambled into his father's arms.

"Ben?" Abe Jenkins called. "Ben boy, you there?"

"He's dead," Caulie answered. "You're next, Jenkins."

Caulie slipped past the shocked Cabots and crept out the back door. Soon he was out amid the darkness, prowling like a cougar in search of a meal. He clubbed one raider senseless, then fired at a nearby rifle flash. A howl of pain rewarded his shot.

"It's time we got clear of this place!" Abe yelled. "There'll be another day."

"They must've got some men in here behind us," another declared. "Let's get!"

Two of the bushwhackers grabbed horses and set off for safety. Matt Simpson ordered them to hold their ground, but it was no use. Four men were already dead, and two others lay wounded. Simpson's band had gotten its fill. They wanted no more of it. One by one they slipped off into the darkness. Finally Matt and the Jenkins brothers departed, too.

"I never thought we'd hold 'em off, Caulie," Marty said as he wrapped linen bandages around Court's bleeding left arm.

"You boys saved the day," Caulie told the shuddering youngster. "Your brother got to me in time, and you, son, held the rear."

"He got past me," Court said, his eyes red with fear and pain. Marty raised the boy's head and gave him a hug.

"He wasn't much trouble by then, boy. Now go open the cellar and let your ma out. She's likely tired of smellin' onions and turnips by now."

Court made his way a foot or so before collapsing. Marty set the boy in a chair and then headed for the cellar door. Caulie knelt beside young Court and listened to the boy's rapid breathing.

"You'll be just fine," Caulie said, brushing a strand of soft blond hair away from the child's forehead. "We'll get you to town. The doc can patch you up just like new."

"Will I have a scar?" Court asked as he stared at the bandaged arm. Blood seeped through the dressing, and Caulie frowned.

"Likely just a bit of one. Big enough to show your friends down at the pond and your grandkids when you're older."

Court tried to smile, but pain flooded the boy's face. As Eve Cabot led a small boy and girl through the door, Caulie swallowed a great bitterness.

"You think you can round us up a horse or two?" Marty asked. "The tack's gone with the barn, but I figure the young ones can ride with us."

"I'll locate some horses," Caulie promised. "You see if you can stop that bleeding. It's best we get him to the doc."

"That means riding past the Simpson place," Eve objected. "Don't you think we can tend it ourselves?"

"It'd be better to have a doc take a look at it," Caulie declared. "You let me worry about Simpson."

"Marty?" she asked.

"I've been followin' this man too many years to head my own way now. Eve, see what clothes and such you can round up. We won't be likely to find much left here when we come home."

She immediately started toward the bedroom. Marty took charge of the children, and Caulie trotted outside to track down the horses. In ten minutes he managed to locate a small chestnut mare and a pinto pony. Marty climbed atop the mare, and Eve took the pony. The smaller children sat in front. Caulie set young Court in front of him atop the black stallion. Then they started for town.

They encountered no difficulty passing the Simpson place. Only a single window showed signs of life, and not a sound drifted through the early morning air. It was a different story in town. A piano played loudly down at one of the saloons, and a trio of cowboys sang along. Caulie headed straight for the doctor, helped Court down, then turned around. He hadn't ridden five feet before the sheriff appeared.

"What's happened here?" the lawman asked. "You've got a lot of nerve riding up here in the middle of the morning."

"Those horses over at the saloon," Caulie said. "They look familiar. Some of 'em might be carryin' the Diamond S brand."

"That's right," the sheriff said. "Matt and some of the boys rode in to celebrate."

"Celebrate?" Caulie asked. "That what skunks like them do when they shoot little kids, burn barns, and terrorize simple folk? They hung Hernando Salazar this afternoon. You know that?"

"Dixon Stewart said as much. I spoke to Matt, but he had ten witnesses swore he was mending a saddle at the time."

"And tonight? I just followed 'em in from the Cabot place. Young Court's got a hole in one arm, and the barn's already a pile of ashes. Can you follow the tracks? There's a clear trail all the way to Marty's place."

"One track's the same as another on that road, Blake. I'll need more'n that to bring a man like Matt Simpson up on charges."

"Ten witnesses you say he had? Check and see which ones of them are lying stone-cold dead at the Cabot place right now. I counted four bodies. Shoot, I'll bet Matt's still got powder smell to his clothes."

"It won't hold water, not in a real trial."

"You mean to do nothin'?" Caulie asked.

"Nothing I can do," the sheriff explained.

"Then I guess it's up to me to settle this business. You have the undertaker get busy. They'll be need of coffins. And markers."

"Blake!"

"I'm tired of seein' my friends and family attacked. There'll be a price paid for tonight. You tell Matt Simpson that!"

"Tell him yourself," young Simpson said, appearing suddenly. "I hear you and your friends have been spreading lies about me. Said I hung some Mex."

"Hernando Salazar was a better man than you'll ever grow to be," Caulie said bitterly. "Now get out of my way."

"You hear him, Sheriff? He's threatening me."

Matt's companions laughed, but the Jenkins brothers backed away a step. Caulie's eyes were suddenly wild, and his fingers tapped the handle of his pistol. Only the sudden arrival of a wide-eyed Charlie Stewart prevented bloodshed.

"Pa says you'd best come along," Charlie whispered. The boy's nightshirt was stuffed into a pair of oversized trousers, and Caulie couldn't help grinning. It broke the tension, and he backed away from Matt and the Jenkins brothers.

"Let's go, Charlie," Caulie said, shoveling the boy along in front of him. "There's been enough death for one night."

Chapter Twelve

Caulfield Blake found Dix's place converted into a small fortress. The neat shelves of goods in the store had been pushed to one wall, allowing room for the displaced Salazars. Marty and Eve had their children spread out in the kitchen, all save little Court, who remained with old Doc Brantley.

"Looks like we've inherited a world of poor relations," Dix remarked as Charlie led Caulie into the parlor. "Pretty soon we'll have half the county here."

"Maybe I should go on back to the cabin," Caulie suggested.

"Not just yet. We've got plans to make. Once the young ones settle down a bit, we'll bed down in Charlie's room. I moved Katie in with Rita so Marty and Eve would have a room to themselves. I don't suppose ole Charlie will mind us imposin' on him. Will you, son?"

"I'll get some blankets," Charlie grumbled. "If there are any left."

"Guess the glamour of cowboyin' took its toll last night," Caulie joked. "A floor can be mighty hard."

"He'd best get used to it. I figure my ranch is next. I'll be goin' out there tomorrow, Caulie. Marty and Roberto will be here to look after the place."

"I figured the Salazars would be halfway to Kansas by now."

"Headed out sure enough, only old man Simpson sent a pair of riders out to badger 'em. Young Carlos took offense and turned the wagon around. He's got a lot of his papa in him, that boy."

"Hope he doesn't end up just as dead."

"It's up to us to see he doesn't."

"And just how do we do that?"

"I figured you'd have a notion, Caulie. You're better at that sort of thing than I am."

Yes, Caulie thought. I am. The solemn look in Dix Stewart's eyes attested to the fact. The two old friends sat down together, and Dix drew out a crude map of the county.

"Here," Caulie said, pointing to a bend in Carpenter Creek. "Simpson's got to go after your place or Hannah's next. No matter which ranch he hits, they'll have to come this way. I remember that place. There's a narrow path alongside the stream that winds past the ridge. Isn't room for more than a couple of men to ride side by side. It winds like the creek, and there's a blind spot perfect for an ambush. A pair of men with rifles could hold off a small army."

"There'll be more than two of you," Marty said, stepping into the parlor. "I figure I have a say in this."

"Others will want to join in, too," Dix said. "To do it right, we'll need everybody who can shoulder a rifle."

"Maybe," Caulie reluctantly admitted. "You think Art and Joe will come along? They can follow orders, and they know when to hold their fire."

"We'll gather everyone tomorrow. You figure Simpson will send his boys out by daylight?"

"If he still has an army," Caulie said, frowning. "We've whittled him down some, though. Even if he sends for help, he's not liable to have all that many experienced riders left. He didn't have enough to take on those farmers at Ox Hollow, and he sure won't have enough to ride down the Bar Double B."

"Then I'd suggest we get ourselves some sleep," Dix said, folding up the map and rising to his feet. "I think we're goin' to need it."

Caulie slept on the floor in a saddle blanket that night. Dix turned restlessly on the bed across the room. Little Charlie slept quietly, but the muffled cries and nightmare screams from the store split the night often. Each time Caulie imagined the terror knifing its way through the small bodies of children who lacked an understanding of the reasons behind the dark cloud of terror that had fallen upon their lives.

Caulie passed the better part of the next morning packing supplies on spare horses. Aside from food there were a half-dozen new Winchesters, together with boxes of shells and sticks of dynamite. A little after noon he prepared to ride out to Dix's cabin above Carpenter Creek.

"We'll be along toward dusk," Dix promised. "Meanwhile, you best have a talk with Marsh. Tell him to keep his eyes open. We could use an extra hand with a rifle tonight, too."

"I'll speak to them."

"You watch out yourself, too. A man like Simpson can have his own tricks. The Jenkins boys are still out there, remember?"

Caulie nodded, then mounted his horse and took the reins of the pack animals. Moments later he was riding eastward down the market road.

The ride to Dix's cabin was the same one Caulfield Blake had made a hundred times, but he'd never taken a path so clouded and dark. The charred timbers of the Cabot barn and the vultures circling above Ox Hollow paid witness to Simpson's outrages. Once Caulfield Blake's heart had filled with laughter and promise as he rode eastward. Now there was only a grim determination fueled by fury.

He hid the packhorses in a ravine behind Dix's cabin and covered the supplies with a blanket and rocks. Once assured all was safely hidden from view, he mounted his horse and headed up Carpenter Creek to the Bar Double B . . . to Hannah and what had once been home.

She met him at the base of the hill. Her eyes were as he always remembered, bright blue like the summer sky and clear as New Orleans crystal.

"There's been more trouble," he told her without dismounting. "It's best I speak with Marsh."

"I'll get him," she said, the smile falling from her face.

"Hannah?"

"Yes?" she asked, staring at him intently.

"You're lookin' well. I think I failed to mention that last time."

"And you look tired."

"Hasn't been much rest of late."

"We saw smoke over to the south. Caleb Cabot rode in last night to warn of riders."

"They burned Marty's barn, shot up the house."

"Eve and the children?" Hannah asked. Her face grew pale, and she swallowed a cry.

"Young Court took a bullet. I got 'em to town. Hernando Salazar's dead. Riders hung him. Roberto and the family are at Dix's."

"Sounds as if he's got a houseful."

"Store's now a barracks."

"It's come down to us, hasn't it?"

"I'd say so."

"Come on along to the house then. I expect you've got serious business to talk over with Marsh."

Caulie nodded and nudged his horse into motion. He followed her slowly. And as he again beheld the house, the porch he had added after the war, the shutters carved from the towering white oaks, he couldn't help feeling hollow. So much had been stolen, the hopes and dreams and expectations that life had once promised. Now he'd come back to find it still there. And yet though he was close enough to touch the planks, he knew Hannah and the future that should have been theirs were beyond his reach.

"Marsh?" she called. "We've got company."

Zach was the first to appear on the porch. He set aside a small barrel and trotted out to greet Caulie.

"Zachary, go fetch your father," Hannah told the boy.

The words had an unintended effect on Caulie and Zach. Both seemed to turn a bit pale, and Caulie's hands trembled. Before either could speak, Marshall Merritt stepped outside.

"Never mind, son," Marsh called. "I heard you, Hannah."

Caulie dismounted. Zach eagerly accepted the reins of the black stallion and smiled up at Caulie.

"I'll see he gets a good, long drink down at the pond," Zach promised, "and a carrot for good measure."

"Thanks," Caulie said, touching the boy's shoulder lightly. He pulled his hand away as he read Marsh's disapproving eyes. Zach seemed equally confused, and Caulie bit his lip in reproval. He'd never intended to muddle things. He wasn't entitled. He'd been away all that time, and Marsh had a right to feel for the boys.

"Why don't we talk inside?" Marsh suggested. "Hannah can make some mint tea."

"I've got some lemons put away," she announced. "I'll make lemonade."

Caulie couldn't help grinning. Lemons rarely made it as far as The Flat. He hadn't tasted lemonade for years. He smiled his appreciation to Hannah, then followed Marsh to the small sitting room that doubled as ranch office.

"So, what news do you bring?" Marsh asked. "Can't be good by the look of you."

"Simpson returned to the hollow. Hung Hernando Salazar. Last night he hit the Cabot place."

"I know. Caleb was here till about an hour ago."

"You're likely next."

"Why so?"

"Not a lot of folks left to choose from. He might try Dix's cabin, but I wouldn't bank on it."

"Thanks for the warning."

"It's more than that. Some of us plan an ambush down at the creek. There's a fine spot for it where the stream bends around that low ridge."

"I know the spot."

"I count on Dix and Marty, Joe Stovall and Art Powell. We might add a few more from town, but it'd be better if we had more rifles."

"It's not rifles you're after," Marsh said, frowning. "You want shooters. We rode with you before. This time if you're wrong, and you've been mistaken before, Hannah and the children could wind up all alone. There are plenty of paths to this place besides the creek road."

"Siler's Hollow is a swamp."

"And the creek trail's a trap. People don't always do as you expect them to."

"I guess not," Caulie said, clearly disappointed.

Hannah arrived with the lemonade, and Caulie sipped his as he pondered what to say next.

"He's planning an ambush, Hannah," Marsh explained. "He wants me to come along."

"And?" she asked.

"I think it best to stay here," Marsh declared.

"Maybe one of the boys . . ." Caulie began.

"No!" Hannah shouted. "I never should've let them go the last time. That was in the daylight. I know you, Caulie. You mean to wait for them in the darkness like you'd wait for Comanches. I won't bury my sons."

"They're my boys, too," Caulie argued. "People will expect them to . . ."

"They're not yours," Marsh said angrily. "You gave up title when you left this place. Wasn't you who stayed up nights nursing their fevers or comforting their hurts."

"I helped 'em get born," Caulie said, shaking. "What's more, I'd see they came to no harm. They mean more to me than . . ."

"Than what?" Carter asked, marching into the room. "Than life? Is that what you were going to say? Then how come you rode off and left us, huh? We're not your sons, not anymore."

"You said that once before," Caulie said, swallowing his own anger as he read Carter's. "Maybe I've earned that. Maybe I haven't. But before you go carvin' me up in your heart, Carter, maybe you ought to consider why I've come back. Not for my health. And if you can't accept me as a father, then at least try to set aside some of that hate. It'll eat you up, just as it's devoured Henry Simpson. I wouldn't wish that on anybody."

"I'll go," Zach offered. "I can shoot pretty fair."

"You couldn't hit a barn from ten feet away," Carter declared. "You'll get yourself killed, Zach."

"No he won't," Hannah said, pulling the boys to her. "Because he isn't going anywhere."

"Ma!" Zach complained. "I know how to keep to the shadows. They shot Court Cabot. Don't tell me I'm too young."

"Do as your ma asks," Caulie said, fighting to control his quivering hands. "Marsh could be right. You might be needed here."

"You don't believe that," Zach said, slipping away from his mother's hands and staring angrily at them all. "I'm not afraid. They'll need help. Ma, is it better for Simpson's men to come here?"

"I think it's time you should leave," Marsh told Caulie. "You brought your warning, and we're grateful for it. As for tonight, we'll keep a sharp watch."

"With luck there'll be nothin' to see," Caulie told them. Then he turned to go. Zach raced over and clung to his arm.

"Pa, you say the word, and I'll meet you at the cabin."

"No, son," Caulie said, gripping the boy's shoulders. "You heard your ma."

"But you need me."

"Maybe she needs you more." Zach shook his head, but Caulie nodded sternly. "Don't look as if you'll never see me again, either. I've got a tough hide. I'll be by again."

"Yes, sir."

"Take care of him, Hannah. He's got heart."

"I will," she promised.

Caulie tried not to think of them as he returned to the cabin. Only now was he realizing how distant they were from his touch.

He was closer to little Charlie Stewart than to his own sons! He scarcely knew Carter at all.

As always when his mind flooded with troublesome thoughts, he turned to work. He passed the late afternoon boarding up shutters and cutting gun notches in the walls. High-caliber rifle bullets fired at close range would penetrate the plank walls, but the oak stood a fair chance of shielding them from anyone firing from a distance.

Caulie recalled how his father had erected rock walls to enclose his old cabin. It had been a fine precaution in days of Indian attack. Caulie regretted Dix hadn't done likewise. The cabin, though stout, would burn like Hernando's cornfield if a bottle of coal oil were tossed upon its roof.

Personally, Caulie didn't expect to fight at the cabin. If the ambush proved successful, Simpson's hooded riders would be finished. Afterward it would be a simple matter to deal with the old man himself, especially if that hothead Matt was in the hands of the sheriff.

Over and over again Caulie envisioned the attack so that when Dix arrived the plan was crystal clear.

"Marsh didn't come?" Dix asked as he and the others climbed down from their horses.

"No," Caulie admitted as he gazed at the weary faces of Dix's companions. Art and Joe were there as expected. Marty Cabot was not. John Moffitt from the livery helped young Carlos Salazar to the cabin. The two youngsters completed the company.

"Not much of a command, eh, Cap'n?" Joe asked. "Four old rebs, a stable boy and a one-armed farm kid."

"We'll do," John declared. "Carlos can still fire his shotgun."

"It'd be more use in town," Caulie argued. "What's become of Marty?"

"His boy took a turn for the worse," Dix explained. "In truth, I don't mind him bein' there with all the womenfolk."

"This isn't goin' to work," Caulie said, shaking his head. "Six isn't enough. Somebody's like as not to get himself killed."

"Yes?" Carlos asked, blinking away pain as he sat on the porch. "They have killed my father, Senor Blake. They've shot me with bullets. Can they do worse? We come knowing the danger. I will fight, and if I must die, then my uncle will see to my mother's needs."

"And you, Joe?" Caulie asked.

"Shoot, Cap'n, I've been shot at by better men than old man Simpson. If somebody don't stop those riders, they'll get around to me and my Sue after a time. It'd grieve me to know I'm not to see her and the girls again, but I figure this is my fight as much as it is yours."

"Me, too," Art added. "I stood with you before, Cap'n. You never led us far wrong."

"What about you, John Moffitt?" Caulie asked. "You forget what Ox Hollow was like? This'll be worse. Night fights always are."

"I hope to ranch this land one of these days," Moffitt said, blushing as Dix's eyes fixed on the young man's face. "Katie and I've got dreams, too. My pa tells me a man fights for his dreams. Is he wrong?"

"No," Dix declared. "I just wish he was along to help."

The others nodded, and Caulie gazed down the creek toward the Bar Double B.

"No point to that, Cap'n," Joe said. "Let's go over the plan and get about it. That young Matt Simpson's been tellin' people at the saloon all afternoon how he wouldn't be surprised if some people were to be sorry for things they've said to the sheriff."

"That's right," Art added. "Said he himself might be busy around dusk."

"Then he's more of a fool that I would've dreamed," Caulie declared. "And he could just be lyin' through his teeth. We'd better get out there early. It's like a Simpson to try a ruse or two."

The ambush site was on Simpson land, and crossing the fences before dark concerned Caulie some. Nonetheless he chose to do so. He set Dix and the others to work building a rock wall across the trail. He and young Moffitt chopped away at the trunk of a tall cottonwood two hundred yards back up the trail. When the riders passed, John would apply the final stroke, and Simpson's raiders would find themselves trapped by the swollen creek, the steep ridge, the rock wall, and the felled cottonwood.

"Then it'll be time to die," Joe Stovall said grimly as he and Art took positions on either side of young Carlos Salazar atop the ridge. Caulie covered John Moffitt near the mouth of the trap. Dix waited behind the stone wall.

And wait they did. It seemed to take an eternity for the sun to drop into the hills to the west. Even then, no riders appeared. Caulie began to worry. Perhaps Marsh was right after all. Maybe Siler's Hollow was passable. It could be that some Diamond S outrider had heard the chopping, or maybe the cut wire had been spotted. A dozen times Caulfield Blake thought of calling the plan off, leading his companions back to the cabin. But in the end they stayed, and finally Matt Simpson led his hooded raiders along Carpenter Creek.

Caulie huddled in the rocks with John Moffitt as the riders galloped past. There were better than a dozen, and all looked ready for fighting. Caulie wished his own little band was half so eager. When the last of them passed, Caulie tapped his young companion on the shoulder. John rose, swung the ax hard, once, twice, a third time. The cottonwood groaned, then crashed earthward, blocking the path like the bar on a prison door.

"Lord, what was that?" one of the raiders shouted.

"Hold up, Matt!" a second yelled.

It was too late. The sharpshooters on the ridge opened fire, and the trail became the deadly trap Caulie intended. Men and horses fell rapidly as the Winchesters fired steadily into the herd of desperate horsemen. One tried to flee through the flooded creek, but Joe Stovall's bullet plucked him from the saddle.

From the ridge the raiders were silhouetted against the faint traces of light outlining the western horizon. Caulie could only distinguish targets as riders approached the fallen tree. The first to come into view called out for others to follow. As the rider stripped away his hood, Caulie smiled grimly. Abe Jenkins was forty feet away when Caulie's Winchester tore the killer from his saddle.

"Abe!" young Matt Simpson cried. John Moffitt fired, but Matt Simpson seemed to lead a charmed life. The bullet killed his horse once again, and Matt tumbled into the creek.

"They're behind that tree!" Matt called to his companions as he swam toward the far bank of the creek. Two horsemen charged, and Caulie was only able to shoot the first. The second managed to hurdle the cottonwood. And in passing, the raider fired his pistol rapidly and to good effect. John Moffitt collapsed as a single bullet sliced through the back of his shoulder and passed into his chest. A second bullet nicked Caulfield Blake's left elbow.

"Boy, you all right?" Caulie asked as he wrapped a bandanna around his own wound. "John?"

Moffitt only groaned in answer, and Caulie was soon too busy to do much anyway. Several riders abandoned their horses and plunged into the creek. One yelped in pain as the marksmen on the ridge let loose a volley. The others managed to escape.

Soon the shooting subsided. Those raiders not among the dead or dying huddled near the rock wall and did their best to return the fire from the ridge. Their leader was clearly Noah Jenkins. Noah was a mere shadow of his brother Abe, though, and the three men with him seemed reluctant to fight it out. Finally Noah made a move toward escape, and Carlos Salazar fired his shotgun. The blast tore the killer apart, and the remaining three raiders cried out for terms.

"Toss your guns aside and raise your hands high!" Dix shouted. "Don't even flinch. We've had enough tricks."

The captive raiders threw down their rifles and raised their arms over their heads. Dix stepped out and took them in hand. Joe and Art then began rounding up the nervous horses and checking the fallen men for signs of life. All but one proved to be dead, and he was bleeding badly from the chest.

Caulie left the others to his companions. He was too busy tearing John Moffitt's shirt into bandages. The young man appeared to have been lucky, for the bullet only narrowly missed a lung. Even so, the bleeding was enough to cause concern.

"Don't worry, son," Caulie said as he worked. "The bullet may have chipped the collarbone a bit, but it passed along through. There'll be no diggin' around for it. And the good Lord gave you some blood to spare."

John did his best to answer, but the young man's face was pale with shock. Caulie tightened the bindings, then carried the wounded stable boy to a waiting horse.

"Joe, Art, get this kid to town," Caulie said anxiously. "He's lost some blood, and the bindings are none too good. Ride fast and hard."

"We know what to do, Cap'n," Joe said, gripping Caulie's arm. "He'll hold together just fine."

"Sure," Caulie agreed. "So what do we do with these three?"

"Sheriff might choose to believe us now," Dix said. "These two I know from way back. They're Diamond S hands. Meet Ernie Lambert and Hollis Scales."

Caulie nodded grimly at the cowboys. They were too frightened to reply.

"Don't know this one," Dix went on to say.

"He held the rope when they hung my father," Carlos said angrily.

Caulie examined the face carefully in the fading twilight. The killer grinned arrogantly.

"His name's Mott," Caulie declared. "He used to ride with the Jenkins brothers."

"That's right," Mott said, laughing. "I remember you, too, Blake."

"Glad to hear you've had some experience with hangings. I expect you'll soon know a good deal more about 'em."

"And just how would that be? We've done nothin' wrong. You come over on Simpson land and ambush us."

"You tryin' to tell us you're just a bunch of poor cowboys?"

Dix asked. "Carlos there can swear you had a hand in his father's hangin'. What's more, you weren't wearin' those hoods for your health, now were you?"

"Sure we were. Right, boys?"

The cowboys nodded. Caulie's fierce stare hushed them, though.

"You might just save your hides if you own up to everything," Caulie declared. "Well? Care to tell the truth?"

"Don't you say a word," Mott commanded. "We have friends. By tomorrow we'll be out on bail. Then we'll see who settles what."

"He could be right," Dix said. Carlos reloaded his shotgun and cocked the hammers.

"You'll never do it, will you, Blake?" Mott taunted. "I know your kind. You're death in a fight, but you've got no stomach for doin' it plain 'n' simple. Go ahead and shoot, boy. Shoot your papa's killers. Well?"

Carlos prepared to fire, but Caulie pulled the shotgun barrel up so that the blast tore into the sky overhead. The cowboys shrank back, but Mott only laughed.

"We'd best get these three to town before I forget myself," Caulie said, glaring at Mott in particular. "I might lose my way and leave young Carlos here alone with the prisoners. It'd be a shame if they made a move to escape."

"A man can sure get himself shot that way," Dix added. "You load that piece up good, Carlos. You feel the urge, I'd hate for the gun not to be ready."

"I was born ready, Senor Stewart," the boy said sourly. "They won't get very far away."

Chapter Thirteen

Caulie sat outside the doctor's house with Marty Cabot as Doc Brantley did his best to sew John Moffitt's torn body back together. Dix and Carlos were still at the jailhouse. Ben Ames, the blacksmith, was there as well, fixing manacles to the legs of the three prisoners.

"I tell you we were on Simpson range, mindin' our very own business," Trandell Mott had argued when Caulie and Dix had presented the trio to the sheriff.

"He had this over his head," Dix had explained, handing over a hood.

"Sheriff, he was one of the men who hung my father," Carlos added.

"You goin' to believe a Mex, Sheriff?" Mott asked.

"Before I'd believe a killer," the sheriff answered. "I've got posters from the New Mexico Territory on you, Mott. A man who's killed once will surely do it again."

Caulie had nodded with grim satisfaction when the sheriff conducted the prisoners to a cell.

* * *

"How's young Court?" Caulie asked as Marty stared at the stars overhead. "Dix said he'd taken poorly."

"He's feverish. Doc says if his arm doesn't improve, it'd be best to take it."

"Lord," Caulie said, bitterly recalling the butchery performed by the surgeons during the war. "Wouldn't seem a bit of fever would merit such action."

"We'll see. Doc hopes openin' up the wound may ease the pain. I hope so. Court's awful little to hurt so much. Did you get 'em all?"

"The Jenkinses. Matt Simpson got away."

"Then nothin's settled," Marty said angrily. "And there'll be worse still to come."

Caulie looked away. He hoped not. He sat there, battle-scarred, bloody, exhausted, for close to an hour. Finally Katherine Stewart stepped outside.

"How is he?" asked Caulie.

"John's asking for food," Kate said, smiling faintly. "Doc says he should stay here tonight. Tomorrow he can come over to our place. I'll tend him till he's well."

"Your place is becomin' a regular hospital," Caulie said, letting her lean against him. "Looks to me like you should go along home yourself. Nothin' much more to do here."

"I'm going to stay with him," she declared. "Doc says I can help tend Court, too. He's going to make me a nurse."

"Well, that sounds like a fair deal to me."

"Uncle Caulie, tell Ma not to worry."

"I'll bet she understands," Caulie said, lifting Kate's chin. "Wasn't so long ago she set her cap for a young man."

She grinned, and Caulie gave her a hug. Then he turned and headed down the street to Dix's place. Before he could knock on the door, Rita stepped out to greet him.

"Kate said to tell you she is stayin' at Doc's tonight," Caulie said. "Holdin' young Moffitt's hand, I suppose."

"Will he be all right?"

"I expect so. He's apt to get good care."

"Yes," she said, smiling. "Caulie, you've got company."

"Me?"

"Yes," she said, leading him along inside. Sitting in the kitchen beside Charlie Stewart and Caleb Cabot was Zach, chewing on a boiled potato.

"Pa, you all right?" the boy said, rushing over and examining Caulie's bandaged elbow.

"What brought you to town, son?" Caulie asked as he led Zach out the door and onto the porch. "Your ma said . . ."

"We heard the shooting," Zach explained. "Was Ma sent me. We, uh, we . . . had to know."

"Sure," Caulie said, staring away a moment.

"You goin' back to the cabin tonight?"

"No, it'd be best not to isolate myself. I'll stay here with Dix. I thought to pay the Simpson place a visit, but we had some prisoners to bring in. John Moffitt needed some tendin', too."

"I should've been along."

"Your ma was right. Could be you over at Doc's right now."

"It might be if you hadn't stopped 'em at the creek. Pa, they're short on space and long on trouble here. Come back with me."

"Your ma send the invitation?"

"She sent me. It's pretty close to the same thing."

"Is it?"

"Pa, when I was really little, I remember talking to you about the war. You were selling horses to the Yanks, and I was all mad about it. Remember?"

"I'm surprised you do. You weren't very big."

"I didn't understand how you could do business with 'em after they killed your own brother. You said something I still remember."

"Oh?"

"You told me somebody has to start mending fences. Don't you think maybe you could do that with Ma?"

"I don't know that we've got fences to mend."

"With Carter then. Lord, he's got himself all tied up in knots about you coming back. He won't even talk to me 'cause I take your side. Ma storms around the kitchen, tossing pots here and there, mad at everybody for no reason."

"That doesn't sound like her."

"It's 'cause she's worried. I know that. She blames herself for getting you in the middle of all this."

"I've been in the middle of this a long time, Zach."

"She asked you to come back, though. There's something more, too. Old man Simpson could come to our place. I got nothing against Marsh. He's been better'n just good to me. Carter's a fair rifle shot, too, but we wouldn't stand much of a chance. I heard all about Court Cabot from Caleb. If anything was to happen to little Sally or Todd or Wylie, I don't know what I'd do."

"You needn't worry about any such thing."

"I do worry. Come home?"

Home? Caulie thought as he gazed into Zach's reddening eyes. Did such a place really exist anymore? Would he be welcome, or would words fly like Hannah's frying pans?

"Pa, please?" Zach pleaded.

"Guess it wouldn't hurt to pass one night there. It's a long ride. You sure you can get me there?"

"Blindfolded," Zach said, jumping up and leaning against Caulie's bloodstained arm. "She'll be glad to see you. You'll see."

Glad wasn't exactly the word for it. Hannah's face bore signs of shock and surprise. As Zach led the horses to the barn, she rushed to his side.

"They've shot you!" she gasped.

"Hardly broke the skin," he told her as she examined the arm. "I wouldn't worry myself, Hannah. I've had worse bein' tossed off an unladylike mustang."

"I know all about that, and I know when somebody's been shot, too."

She conducted him inside the house, removed the bandanna, and scrubbed the wound. After fixing him a cup of mint tea and stuffing a thick slice of bread down him, she ordered Carter to drag out the bathtub once again.

"I'm too tired for all this fuss, Hannah," Caulie complained.

"Tired or no, I won't have you fester up on me."

"I can take my own bath."

"Don't let it bother you, Pa," Zach said, gazing in through the doorway. "She bosses everybody that way, and she bathes us all right in front of everybody."

"Not me," Caulie objected. "It's not proper. We'll do it in the kitchen. And what help I might need Zach can provide."

"Zach needs his rest," Hannah told them. "Get to your bed, young man. As to your privacy, Caulie Blake, there's not much I haven't seen before, and more than once I might add."

Zach laughed loudly, and Carter dragged the bathtub in.

"Boys, see if you can get him out of those rags. I'll bet Marsh has something he can wear."

"Ma, remember that old trunk in the storeroom?" Zach said. "It's full of Pa's old clothes. Some likely still fit. He hasn't put any weight on."

"Probably not," Hannah agreed. "I've tasted his cooking. I wouldn't feed it to pigs."

"Now hold on," Caulie complained. "I seem to recall you took a likin' to my berry pies."

"Well, you did have a way with baking, I grant. But what you did with meat stands as a crime."

He laughed at her, and for a second the last seven years seemed to fade off into memory. Then he spotted Carter's disapproving face and grew silent. Hannah saw it, too.

"Ma, the little ones are waiting for you to hear their prayers," Carter said. "Pa's been in there awhile, biding time till you came."

"Then I'd best go along," she said. "The boys can start the water boiling."

"Sure," Zach said as he took down a kettle from the wall and headed for the water barrel. Carter turned away, but Caulie reached out and held the boy in place.

"Don't you think it's time we made our peace, Carter?" Caulie asked. "I don't think I can bear to read so much hatred in your eyes."

"When you leave, you won't have to see it anymore," Carter said, shaking loose.

"That's true. Is that all I should remember?"

Carter stopped a second. He turned slowly and stared sadly at Caulie.

"You didn't have too much trouble forgetting the last time."

"I didn't?" Caulie asked, his eyes growing wide. "You boys were never out of my thoughts. I wrote, often and steady."

"Letters," Carter grumbled. "What use's a letter? You don't know how it was, all the people calling you names, saying you were a coward and a traitor, siding with the Yanks and all. Ma quit sending us to school in town. 'Cept for Kate Stewart, I had no friends. Ma wasn't even welcome at church."

"It was hard on me, too," Caulie said as he unbuttoned his bloody shirt. "I lay on my back three days. Then I rode as far north as I could. Even so, for six months each time I saw a stranger, I figured he was sent by Henry Simpson."

"We even changed our names!" Carter cried.

"That's a lot to ask a man to do," Caulie said, gazing at the floor. "But not as much as to ask him to give up his wife, his family, his home. Seven years is a long time, Carter, and I won't ask forgiveness. Only know for each hour of pain you've felt, I've known two. And many's the time I've thought I'd been better off if Simpson's hirelings'd finished me that night in town."

"I never wished for that," Carter said, sitting beside Caulie on the floor. "But you brought down such hard times on us."

"Not me," Caulie objected. "Henry Simpson. And now he's started again. It's time he paid."

"Men like Simpson never pay," Carter said bitterly. "They hire the work done, or they buy off judges."

"He didn't the last time," Caulie declared. "And he won't this time, either. We won't settle our business in a courtroom. It's bound to come to a head soon, and the final word will be spoken out there among the same rocks and hills and creeks we've fought over for fifteen years."

"Who will win?" Zach asked, returning with the water.

"I guess we'd better," Caulie said as Zach lit a fire and filled a kettle with water.

By the time the water was hot and the tub was full, Caulie had shed his clothes and settled into the bath. The swirling warmth chased off some of the shivers that had plagued him since the ambush. The reluctant approval in Carter's eyes had done the rest.

"Time you boys were in your blankets," Hannah announced as she returned to the kitchen.

"I left you a nightshirt there on the chair," Zach explained before going. "Carter and I'll carry the rest to our room. It all right if he beds down with us, Ma?"

"If he can stand the strain of four boys inside four walls."

"Can't be too much worse'n winterin' with a half-dozen buffalo hunters," Caulie said.

Hannah laughed and waved the boys out the door. Then she grew more serious.

"Marsh is none too happy you're here," she told him. "I just couldn't see shunting you off to Dix's cabin, hungry and wounded and all."

"There's a month's food in that cabin," Caulie said, "and it's far from uncomfortable. It might be better I was gone tomorrow."

"Better for who?"

"Everybody, especially you, Hannah. I never meant to come between you and Marsh. I must've been a fool to've hoped I could get to know Carter and Zach again without it makin' things hard on Marsh. He's been a good husband?"

"The best."

The answer stung, and Caulie busied himself a moment with the scrubbing.

"Carter told me how hard it was for you," Caulie told her. "You never let on."

"Would it have changed anything, Caulie? I don't imagine you had an easy time yourself."

"No."

"And now you've come back. There've been a lot of changes."

"I know. Carter's close to as tall as Lamar was when we raided that depot in Tennessee. As tall as he ever got to be."

"What will happen next, Caulie? Which way will it turn?"

"Depends on Simpson, Hannah. And the sheriff. I've known lots of lawmen, though, and this one doesn't seem to have the stomach for a set-to with Henry Simpson."

"So he'll come."

"Here or maybe to town. He's lost some men. Might be easier to bring somebody in with an itch to set fires."

"One spark and the whole town would go up. Don't forget. Henry Simpson owns most of that town. He'd hardly celebrate if the hotel burned down."

"Might be worth it to rid himself of Dix and the others."

"He could do that just as easily by burning us out."

"Then it's likely that's what he'll choose to do."

She started to say something more, but he put a finger to his lips. Little Wylie stood in the doorway, and Hannah turned her attentions to the child. The water was growing tepid, and Caulie rose slowly. He wrapped a nearby towel around himself, then sat in a chair and rubbed the soreness from his weary body.

"I meant to help you with that," Hannah said.

"You're needed elsewhere," Caulie said, nodding to a confused Wylie. "I'll tend to myself."

"But the arm . . ."

"I've dressed wounds before," Caulie assured her. "I'll see you at breakfast."

She seemed a bit disappointed, but she didn't argue. Instead she led Wylie off, leaving Caulie to dry himself. It took but a few moments, and he draped the nightshirt Zach had left him over a pair of tired shoulders and set off down the hall.

118

Caulie had no trouble finding the boys' room. After all, he and his father had built most of the house. The only change in the room was that the small beds that had once occupied the far wall had been moved to the opposite wall. Two larger beds replaced them. Between the beds lay a quilt Hannah's mother had made from scraps of wool uniform coats left from the war. Underneath that quilt Zach was deep in sleep. Carter lay on the near bed, his eyes wide open.

"He said you'd appreciate the comfort of a real bed," Carter whispered, pointing to his sleeping brother. "Zach could sleep on a fencepost."

"Not always," Caulie said as he sat on the bed and drew the blanket aside. "He used to curl up in a little ball on my lap. Then when I'd place him in his bed, he'd kick like a Missouri mule."

"He stopped doing that a long time ago."

"Sure," Caulie said, sliding beneath the covers. "Seven years changes things."

"Yes, it does," Carter said somberly. "What am I supposed to call you? How can we explain you to Todd and Wylie and Sally? Am I Carter Merritt still or am I a Blake again?"

"All that'll sort itself out, son."

"That's it in a nutshell. Am I your son? Was Marsh helped me use a razor the first time. He bought me a rifle and taught me to shoot. Am I supposed to forget all that?"

"Don't ever forget any of the good things," Caulie advised. "Try to forgive the bad. My pa told me that when I was just about your age, Carter. I do my best at it."

"You haven't forgiven Simpson."

"No, I haven't," Caulie confessed.

Caulie closed his eyes and let Carter do likewise. But tired though he was, Caulie couldn't seem to find any rest. He kept gazing at his sons, two lean figures with long legs and broadening shoulders. It didn't seem possible. When they spoke, manly sounds flowed from their lips. Carter was using a razor! Was it possible so much time had passed? Seven years. It was a terribly long time, longer even than the war, and that had lasted an eternity. All those months and days alone, drifting rootless on the wind, had taken their toll.

It was too long, Caulie told himself. He'd never drift like that again. No, death was better than being alone.

Chapter Fourteen

Caulie woke to the sound of an ax chopping kindling. The sun was well up in the eastern sky, and he was surprised to have slept so late. The other beds in the little room were deserted. Blankets were neatly tucked beneath mattresses, and Zach's bedding was carefully stacked atop a small trunk at the foot of the bed. An ancient pair of woolen trousers and a homespun shirt lay there as well.

"Well, I'll be," Caulie muttered as he pulled aside his covers and rolled to the end of the bed. "My old chest."

As he bent over to examine it, his stiff elbow ached. He went ahead anyway. The initials C.B. were hand lettered on the tough leather sides, and Caulie knew all too well what lay inside. A cavalry saber, two Colt dragoon model pistols, a brace of aging flintlocks brought out west by his grandfather, and the remains of a Confederate officer's coat occupied the bottom. On top were clothes left behind, neatly stored away in hope of Caulie's return.

"I always figured you'd be back for that trunk," Hannah said, stepping into the room. "Guess it's a good thing I saved it."

"A relic from the past," Caulie told her. "The clothes'll come in handy now. The guns belong in a travelin' show. They're just curiosities now."

"They're a legacy. My boys will want them someday."

"I don't know that I'd bet my house on that, Hannah. Carter doesn't have much use for me."

"Is that why he spent an hour shining your boots? You always were a mite quick to judge, Caulie. Give them time. They passed a lot of sunsets staring down at the creek, expecting you to ride home from your wanderings."

"I was told I wouldn't be any too welcome."

"I was tired of gazing down that road, Caulie."

"I guess a woman has a right to a husband who stays at her side."

"She does."

"I wish I could've been one, Hannah. Wanderin' sure seems to have levied a heavy price."

"On all of us," she said sadly. "If you're hungry, I can fry you some ham, a couple of eggs. . . ."

"Easy up?" he asked, grinning.

"Easy up," she echoed, returning his smile.

He nodded, and as she headed for the kitchen, he shed his nightshirt and dressed himself. The trousers smelled of mothballs and gun grease, and the shirt fit poorly. They were clean, though, and he'd worn worse.

Caulie smoothed out some of the wrinkles, then joined Hannah in the kitchen. She was busy frying eggs and merely pointed to a chair. He sat down, and minutes later she handed him a platter of ham with two sizzling eggs on top.

"Well?" she asked as he took the first bite.

"Like old times," he said, smiling.

"Yes," she said with a sigh. She then returned to the stove and set a kettle on to boil.

Caulie saw the distress etched into her face. He knew he'd put it there. He started to speak, but the words wouldn't come. Instead he finished his breakfast in silence.

Later he walked along the hill to Carpenter Creek. Zach was there skipping flat stones across the swollen stream. Hannah's three little ones huddled together beside their older brother and watched. Caulie thought to join them, but the strange uneasiness filling the twins' eyes stopped him. Only the girl seemed friendly. She flashed a good-natured smile in Caulie's direction, and he nodded in answer.

He had a notion to soak his weary feet in the cool water and rest his aching arm, but the sound of an approaching rider cast everything from Caulie's mind.

"Pa?" Zach asked, racing over.

"Best get the little ones up the hill, son," Caulie warned. By the time Zach chased the twins and Sally back to the house, Marsh and Carter appeared atop the hill armed with shotguns. Only one rider splashed his way down Carpenter Creek, though, and Caulie recognized the scrap of ill-fitting cloth and unkempt blond hair as Charlie Stewart.

"Mr. Blake," the boy cried, drawing his horse to a halt and gesturing wildly back toward town. "There's been trouble in town."

"What manner of trouble?" Caulie asked. "Your ma and pa are all right?"

"Yes, sir," the boy said as he struggled to catch his breath. "Mostly." ·

"What happened?"

"Was Colonel Simpson's boys. Nobody saw 'em clearly, but we all know. They raided the jailhouse first."

"Freed the prisoners?"

"In a way," Charlie said grimly. "Killed 'em, every last one."

"Good Lord," Marsh said, shaking his head as he joined Caulie beside the tired young messenger.

"I guess Simpson's not takin' any chances on a trial," Caulie mumbled. "Well, there must be more, Charlie. Dix didn't send you out here without a fair purpose. Ridin' these hills alone's not the wisest thing a man could do."

"They didn't just go to the jailhouse," Charlie said, staring off into the distance as he tried to swallow a mixture of fear and rage. "They came to the store, tore down the door, then started after Pa. They beat him up. Locked Carlos in the storeroom and pinned me to the floor. We'd helped if we could've. Mr. Cabot and Caleb heard the ruckus and came over. Heaven sent, they were. One look at Mr. Cabot's rifle sent them cowboys runnin'."

"How's Dix?"

"Fair," Charlie said. "Ma says town's too dangerous. She put Pa in a wagon and took him to the ranch. The Cabots stayed in town, what with Court still hurt and all. Katie stayed to look after Johnny Moffitt. The Salazars went with Ma."

"I'll be out to help organize things," Caulie promised. "You tell your pa not to hurry himself to his feet."

"He's not one to listen to such advice from me," Charlie said, stabbing his chest with a thumb. "Might from you, though."

"I'll saddle my horse. Charlie, are Joe and Art well?"

"They stayed in town, too. Looked scared, though."

Caulie frowned. Things had quickly taken a turn for the worse. That was certain.

"Charlie, would you like some breakfast?" Hannah called to the youngster.

"Couldn't eat a thing," Charlie said, shaking his head. "Thank you, ma'am. I'd best get along back."

"Wait for me," Caulie urged. "I won't be long."

He started immediately for the barn. Hannah raced over to argue, but Caulfield Blake wasn't a man who changed his mind once he set it to a course.

"He knows best, Hannah," a relieved Marsh declared. "The danger's upstream."

"I know that well enough!" she raged. "You can't let him follow that boy up there and get himself killed. Caulie, Charlie, bring the others here. We can hold out together."

Marsh shook his head, and Caulie nodded. Dix would never come anyway. The fight had come to his land, and he'd never been one to take the first step in a retreat.

It took but a few minutes for Caulie to ready his horse. The stallion seemed to sense the urgency in Caulie's movements, and the big horse stomped the ground in anticipation. As he smoothed out the saddle blanket and lifted his dusty saddle onto the horse's broad back, Caulie noticed he had company. Carter pushed Zach inside the barn, and the two boys stared up solemnly into their father's eyes.

"Ma'd have you stay," Carter spoke. "You heard her."

"In time," Caulie answered. "Just now it's hard . . . on all of us."

"Pa?" Zach asked.

"Please, son, no good-byes," Caulie pleaded. "There've been enough of 'em already, and besides, I'll come back."

"Will you?" Carter questioned.

"I always have," Caulie assured them. "Look after your ma."

Caulie tightened the cinch, stroked his horse's neck, and mounted. He rode past the boys, past a sad-eyed Hannah, and along to where Charlie Stewart anxiously waited.

"Ready?" the boy asked.

"Lead on, Charlie," Caulie said, pausing only to wave faintly at the family that he was once again leaving behind. He promised himself it wouldn't be years this time, though. Not if he could help it.

Chapter Fifteen

Dix's cabin was a beehive of activity. Roberto Salazar had his family busy felling trees for a makeshift shelter. Rita supervised the unloading of a wagonload of supplies, cooking implements, and clothing. Dix sat on the porch and drank it all in. His bandaged head and bruised face ignited a fire in Caulie's chest.

"I was a fool to have believed it could be otherwise," Dix said as Caulie dismounted. "You've got the spare guns hidden?"

"Close by. I wish we'd used the dynamite to blast old man Simpson to perdition, though."

"More likely got you shot. Well, when they come, we'll be ready."

"Will we, Dix? Or will it be another Ox Hollow? You'd been safer in town."

"I'd only brought trouble there. Besides, there are too many shadows. We hold the high ground here. And don't forget. There aren't as many of 'em left now."

"Oh, I don't know," Caulie said, rubbing his whiskered chin. "Men the likes of Abe and Noah Jenkins can always be found if you search the right places . . . and offer enough gold."

"I hope you're wrong."

But Caulfield Blake wasn't often mistaken, and this time was no exception. Even as the Stewarts and Salazars settled in at the cabin, Henry Simpson had riders scouting the countryside. Fences were cut, and cattle grazing on Stewart range were run up Carpenter Creek to the Diamond S. Matt Simpson boldly rode up to the cabin door with a bill of sale.

"You've got to be crazed!" Dix cried.

"Call it justice," Matt declared. "You've killed Simpson people. You drowned a quarter of our livestock. Just sort of evens things out."

Caulie rode over to the Bar Double B that night and discovered much the same there.

"A man who'd steal your water and your home isn't apt to mind stealin' some stock," Marsh said. "Not much we can do. The Simpson's've always got somebody watchin' the house. They ride in threes or fours, well-armed and eager to shoot. If I took Carter, or even him and Zach both with me, those buzzards would swoop down on the house in the blink of an eye. What chance would Hannah and the little ones have? No, they know they've got us in a bind."

"Yes," Caulie agreed.

Soon things grew worse. Simpson posted riders on the road. It was impossible to get word in and out of town, much less supplies. When Katie Stewart tried to bring out a load of flour and ammunition, Simpson cowboys sent her walking barefoot back to town.

Perhaps for that reason Caulie was filled with uneasiness when Marty Cabot appeared one day with a wagon full of provisions. New rifles, shotgun shells, and two boxes of Winchester cartridges were hidden beneath trunks of clothing and boxes of cornmeal and assorted food tins.

"I went by way of Ox Hollow, then cut down an old trace east of my house," Marty explained. "Likely they didn't spot me."

"Maybe not there," Caulie said, "but they always have a man or two watchin' us. I don't like it much. You could've got yourself shot real proper, Marty."

"Couldn't be helped," Marty explained. "I figured you needed the goods. I brought word on young Moffitt, too. He's better. Gettin' downright feisty with young Kate."

"And Court?" Charlie asked.

"Be a time yet 'fore he's chasin' you round any creeks, Charlie Stewart," Marty said, smiling faintly. "He's takin' solid food, though, and the swellin' goes down each day. Evie's still a bit worried, but the boy'll mend. He's a Cabot."

"Sheriff still sittin' atop that fence of his?" Dix asked. "Or has he sent word of what's goin' on to somebody?"

"Telegraph's down," Marty told them. "As for the sheriff, nobody's seen him in two days. Word is he took a huntin' trip up north. Maybe to Kansas."

"The only man with a brain in this whole county," Rita remarked. "Simpson will have a man wearin' that badge once he finishes with us."

"He hasn't done that yet," Caulie reminded her.

"Oh? I wonder why?" Rita asked. "Sure isn't for love of any of us."

"He's prolongin' the pain," Caulie explained. "I know him. He enjoys this. But it could turn on him again. It has before."

"Caulie, stop it!" Rita cried. "Look at us! We're holed up here like scared rabbits. We need help. What use are a few tins of beans and a sack of cornmeal? There are children here! What about Katie and the Cabots in town? Hannah and Marsh down the creek? Who's next?"

"I don't know," Caulie confessed. "I do know Marty's not ridin' back to town by himself."

"I'll go," young Carlos Salazar offered.

"You've got a bad arm and a mama to look after," Caulie objected. "I'm the one to do it."

"And who'll return with you?" Dix asked.

"I've ridden worse places alone," Caulie said with a coldness that chilled his companions. "Why don't I take along a couple of sticks of dynamite, Dix? Might find some use for 'em."

"Caulie, you be careful," Rita said, grasping his arm.

"I always am," Caulie told her, smiling. "You keep an eye out, Dix. They could come up here anytime."

"I know what to do," Dix answered. "Once the wagon's unloaded, we'll be set."

Caulie would have preferred waiting for darkness before starting back toward town with Marty, but delaying would give Simpson time to make plans. The old man was bound to know about Marty's trip. A wagon cut a wide path, and the return trip would offer a hundred chances at ambush.

"It'd be better to borrow a horse, leave that blamed wagon," Caulie advised.

"It'll be needed later," Marty explained. "Supplies won't last forever. I'd guess the Bar Double B's growin' short, too. Better for us to make the trip from town than for you to come both ways."

"You'd have to go back, Marty, just like now."

"Next time we come, we'll be ridin' out here to stay," he declared. "Doc Brantley's basement's hardly a place to rear a family."

"Could be a lot safer."

"So maybe Evie and the little ones'll stay. I'll bring Caleb along. He's a fair shot."

"This isn't a fight for children," Caulie argued. "Marty, there've been enough killed."

"Too many."

Caulie nodded. He started to reply when a rifle spoke instead. The bullet splintered the wagon, and Marty instinctively slapped the horses into a gallop. Up ahead a pair of shotgun-toting cowboys stood and fired. The horses reared in terror, but though the blast shattered the air, the animals continued on unharmed. The rifle barked again, though, and Marty slumped across the wagon seat.

"No!" Caulie screamed, pulling his pistol and charging into the tangle of briars and oak saplings where the bushwhacker was hiding. A man stepped out of the way of Caulie's horse, but Caulie managed to slam the barrel of the pistol against the rifleman's forehead. The impact sent the would-be killer flying, and Caulie turned his horse toward the two fleeing figures to his left. As they discarded their shotguns and raced toward waiting horses, a fourth bushwhacker appeared. The dark-browed killer's daunting eyes and easy step halted Caulie's progress. Olie Swain was well-known as a road agent and hired killer up in Young County.

"Don't stop now, Blake," Swain called as he slithered through the trees, his face half hidden by the barrel of a shiny Winchester. "You're worth two hundred dollars to me."

"Oh?" Caulie asked, sliding off his horse and darting behind a boulder as Swain fired. "Doesn't seem like much to get yourself killed for."

"You know how it is," the outlaw taunted Caulie as he fired a second shot over his head. "Railroads carry all the cash nowadays. Stage doesn't offer much to a man. Who knows? This Simpson fellow says he might even make me sheriff once you're dealt with."

"Might be a long wait, Olie," Caulie declared as he concentrated on the broken ground just ahead. Marty's wagon was caught in a tangle of brush two hundred yards down the trail. The horses were close to panic, and Marty was yet to show a sign of life. Swain was somewhere off to the right, slowly and cautiously closing the distance.

Caulie cursed himself for not plucking the Winchester from its saddle scabbard. The Colt was little good firing at any distance, especially through the maze of oaks and junipers.

"Where've you gotten to, Blake?" Swain asked. "Not dead already, I hope. I haven't had any sport from this."

You will, Caulie thought as he moved out from the rocks. A rifle shot sent him flying to the ground. Two more tore limbs from trees just overhead. Caulie dragged himself down a wash, then turned and waited. Swain's rifle followed, tracing Caulie's movements with a trail of bullets. Swain himself remained a shadow.

Just ahead a nervous rattlesnake warned of its presence. The warm sandstone rocks at the base of the gully were a natural haven for snakes. Caulie took a deep breath and gazed first at the wagon, then back toward Swain.

You're good, Olie, Caulie silently told his tormentor. But this is my game, and I'm good at it. Instead of continuing his retreat toward the wagon, Caulie climbed the steep bank of the ravine and slowly, silently nestled into a natural depression atop the embankment. Moments later Swain darted along the opposite slope. The killer appeared momentarily confused. Caulie thought to fire, but Swain bobbed like a cork on a windswept creek. The movement startled the rattlesnakes, and they stirred restlessly.

"Down that ravine, are you?" Swain finally called, firing wildly down the slope. The outlaw then jumped, landing but a foot from the rocks. Instantly a rattler sprang out, striking Swain's upper leg. A second and a third struck also, sinking their venomous fangs into Swain's arm and side.

"Ahhh!" the gunman cried, shaking off the snakes as another and another crawled out of its lair, each adding its deadly bite. Caulie turned away. He'd known a snakebit man to thrash around in agony for hours. But as the snakes continued to strike out at Swain's writhing arms and legs, adding each time to the poison surging toward the killer's dark heart, the end was not far away.

Caulie had other matters to attend. He found Marty groaning beside the wagon. A bullet had opened up a nasty hole in Marty's left thigh.

"Looks like you won't be goin' anywhere save Doc Brantley's," Caulie said as he tightened the tourniquet Marty had already begun. "Bleedin's stopped. Think you can crawl into the back of this wagon?"

"If you'll lend a hand," Marty said, paling as Caulie helped him into the wagonbed.

"I'm only goin' to back the horses a bit," Caulie said, leading the frantic team out of the dense underbrush. He then steadied the horses and called out to his own mount. The gunshots had sent the big black flying, though, and Caulie reluctantly left the tall stallion to find its own way.

"That was Olie Swain back there," Marty said as Caulie climbed into the seat and got the team headed back down the trail toward the market road.

"Seems the price on our hides is goin' up."

"You shot him?"

"No, some friends tended to him."

"Friends?"

"Rattlesnakes. He's just as dead, though." Caulie assured his old friend. "For now, rest up and watch that leg."

Marty nodded, and Caulie concentrated on keeping the jarring to a minimum. The trail was rough and rock-strewn, though, and more than once Marty cried out in pain as the wagon bounded in and out of a hole or over a small boulder.

Once they reached the market road, Caulie left caution to the wind. He set the horses to a gallop, hoping the rapid motion might allow him to escape Simpson's roving eyes.

Lord, I've asked a lot of you of late, Caulie prayed silently, but this is a good man I've got back of me. He's bleeding, and he doesn't need another tangle with Henry Simpson just now. Get us through this, won't you?

Caulie glanced behind him and saw Marty was doing much the same. Perhaps the prayers were answered, for the only sign of life they encountered during the wild four-mile scramble down the road toward town was a lone cowboy near the gate to the Diamond S.

"Hold up there!" the drover called. "Hold up!"

Caulie never hesitated. He slapped the horses onward, then fired a shot as the cowboy started to pursue. The rider halted immediately, and the wagon rushed past undaunted.

When they reached town, Caulie slowed the wagon. He headed directly for Dr. Brantley's house. The doctor emerged from the house, grinning, but the smile faded as he read the panic on Caulie's face.

"You're keepin' me in business, Caulfield Blake," the doctor complained.

"No, this is Henry Simpson's handiwork," Caulie said bitterly. "It's apt to get rewarded."

"Well, before you do anything else, give me a hand with Marty. Lord, I'm runnin' short of beds."

"Yes," Caulie said with a frown. And it was likely to grow worse.

While the doctor treated Marty's leg wound, Caulie sat on a bench outside the house and tried to catch his breath. That last tension-filled hour and a half had taken a toll. He couldn't help wondering what might have happened had not the wash sheltered a nest of rattlesnakes. So often life and death hung on the barest thread of chance.

"Uncle Caulie?" Kate Stewart whispered, breaking him out of his stupor.

"Kate?" he replied, gazing up at her melancholy eyes.

"Are my folks . . . Charlie . . . are they all right?"

"Well, Dix's mendin' well enough. Your ma misses you, but the work keeps her occupied. As for Charlie, well, he's half range mustang and the other half creek mud and river rat. They worry for you and young John."

"He's better. I thought to join them. Maybe you could . . ."

"It's better you stay in town," Caulie told her. "Eve's likely to need help just now."

"It's going to get worse, isn't it?"

"Maybe. But things are drawin' to a head. Won't be long before we settle this."

"Yes," she agreed, taking his hand and squeezing it tightly. "But when it's settled, will any of us be left?"

"I trust so."

"I always thought myself brave," Kate said, sighing. "But if it were up to me, I'd give Colonel Simpson anything he wants so long as he promises to leave my family alone."

"That's how men like Simpson grow," Caulie explained. "They prey on the weak and the disorganized. When he came here, he played on our sympathies, talked of dreams and ideals. Emma Siler sold him land cheap. My pa loaned him stock. Then when the war came, he spoke of patriotism and duty, sent two of his boys off to fight with me and your pa in the cavalry. While we were gone, he bought up land, forced neighbors out of business, grabbed every acre of land left to widows and orphans who had nothin' else to sell for food money.

"Those who saw it happenin' always thought to let things lie. Comanches were a bigger threat. Then the Yanks. So Simpson gobbled up one after another of the small ranches. Then when war ended and we came back, he set his enemies onto the Yank garrisons."

"He's good setting people against each other. Pa told me what happened to you."

"And now, when folks begin to see what's happenin', there aren't many of us left to do anythin'."

"He's not won yet."

"No, he hasn't," Caulie declared. "It's not over yet, not by half."

Doc Brantley emerged from the house then, and Caulie turned his attention to the surgeon.

"I got the bullet," the doctor explained, "but the wound bled freely. He could still lose that leg if he rushes it."

"There's no need of that," Caulie assured him. "If you're short of space, I'm sure I can persuade Joe Stovall or Art Powell to make room."

"It's best he stay with me for now. I've got Court in there anyway. Eve and the little ones don't take up much space."

"Thanks, Doc," Caulie said, shaking the doctor's weary hand. "It's not altogether healthy to cross Henry Simpson these days."

"You keep that in mind yourself, Caulfield Blake. Bullets don't pay much heed to reputation."

Caulie nodded. He might have continued the conversation a bit longer had not a trio of horses thundered down the street. Caulie turned instantly in that direction. Without thinking, he gripped his pistol.

"Pa?" Zach called out as he jumped off the bay mare and stumbled against his father's side. "Pa?"

Dix Stewart and young Charlie arrived seconds later. Charlie grinned and gave a nod to his sister. It was Dix who spoke.

"What happened? Lord, Caulie, that big black stallion of yours came trottin' back to Hannah's. The rifle was still in its sheath. We thought you bushwhacked for certain."

"Not me," Caulie explained. "Marty. It was a close thing."

"Marty?" Dix asked. "He's not . . ."

"No," the doctor answered. "But I'd recommend you fellows quit offerin' targets to Henry Simpson's guns."

"We'll keep that in mind, Doc," Dix said, embracing his daughter, then turning back to Caulie. "Long as we're all in town, we've got need of more supplies."

"Won't be easy gettin' a wagon by Simpson's boys again," Caulie argued. "Maybe we should pack some horses."

"I've got two mules at the livery," Dr. Brantley offered. "John Moffitt's not apt to need his horse, either."

"Tom's got a string of fair saddle mounts, too," Dix said, gazing down the street. "I'll see what I can round up in the way of supplies back at the store. Caulie, you collect the horses. I'd just as soon get back as quick as possible."

"Yes," Caulie agreed, turning to Zach. "Son, what brought you along?"

"You did," Zach replied. "That black came back to *our* place. Ma said to ride out and see what had happened. She never said how far."

"But I suspect she'll be vexed that you came to town. It could prove dangerous."

"I've been shot at before. Remember, Pa?"

Caulie thought to explain how it would be different this time, riding through country knowing every rise of ground, every boulder-strewn gully might conceal an ambush. But Zach's eyes were full of the fires of adventure, of youthful daring. There was no room for caution. Caulie was glad the boy wouldn't be riding alone.

"Guess we'd best get about our business," Caulie finally said. "Charlie, why don't you help your pa with those supplies. Zach here can . . ."

"Help *my* pa," Zach finished, grabbing Caulie's arm and leading the way toward the livery.

It took Caulie a quarter of an hour to round up Doc Brantley's mules, young John Moffitt's pony, and a packhorse Joe Stovall could spare. Caulie also talked Stovall out of three fresh saddle horses, one each for Dix, Charlie, and himself. Zach agreed straightaway to ride Moffitt's mustang. Loading the mules and the packhorse with the supplies took slightly longer. After assuring himself Marty would mend and allowing Dix to fill Kate in on her mother's well-being, Caulie led the small caravan eastward along the market road.

"I'd sure feel better swingin' south toward Ox Hollow," Dix declared. "Seems like we're askin' for it, headin' right past Simpson's front door as we are."

"Maybe," Caulie admitted, "but Marty couldn't slip through, and it's his own land we'd have to cross. I'd rather face Simpson with fresh horses and a shorter distance. Besides, you know they've got somebody watchin' the cabin."

"I know," Dix said, glancing at the boys. "It's just that we're not ridin' the back country, scoutin' Yanks this time, Caulie. We've got . . ."

"Yes," Caulie said, cutting his old friend short. "But I couldn't see leavin' them in town."

"Leavin' who?" Charlie asked.

"You," Zach said, slapping his young companion across the knee. "You don't have to worry about us, Mr. Stewart. Charlie and I can outride anybody on the Simpson payroll."

"You can't outride a bullet!" Dix told them sternly. "Just do as you're told, and if we run into trouble, head for the ranch. Fast. And don't worry about us. Zach, your pa and I were tanglin' with bushwhackers before you were born."

It wasn't bushwhackers that blocked the trail, though. Fifty yards short of the Diamond S front gate Matt Simpson waited on horseback. He held a Winchester across his knee. Four cowboys flanked him. Caulie recognized one as Doyle Opley, a Kansan famed for his talents with a Sharps carbine, a deck of cards, and a running iron. Ranchers along the Brazos had posted a $500 reward on him.

"Well, look what we've stumbled across," Opley said, laughing as Matt raised his rifle. "Seems your grandpa was right, Matt. These scrub-brush ranchers've lost their caution."

"That can get a man real dead," Matt said, grinning as he fired the rifle over Dix's head. The horses reared up, and Caulie struggled to hold on to the leaders for the mules.

"You that eager to die?" Caulie asked, waving for Charlie and Zach to head along down the road. Neither moved.

"Blake, you don't understand, do you?" Matt asked. "You're done for. You won't slip through our fingers this time."

"I suspect that's what Olie Swain thought, too," Caulie said coldly. "Found him yet?"

"We found him," one of the cowboys said. "Ran afoul of a snake."

"Yeah," Caulie said, grinning cruelly. "Was real enjoyable. I led him right down into those rattlers."

Matt's smile faded, and Caulie eased his pistol out of its holster.

"Olie was a good man," Opley declared. "But he wasn't long on thinkin'."

"He's got a long time to think on things now," Caulie said, motioning again for the boys to move on. "An eternity."

"Enough talk," Matt Simpson said angrily. "Let's get this over."

"Matt, two of 'em's just boys," a cowboy argued.

"Now!" young Simpson shouted.

The first cowboy reached for a pistol, and Caulie shot him dead.

"Go!" Caulie yelled, tossing the leaders aside and kicking his horse into a gallop. Zach slapped the mules into motion, then chased them eastward. Charlie followed, and Dix pulled the packhorse along behind him. Caulie followed, then turned back to block the path of Simpson's riders. Matt was firing wildly at the departing horses, and Doyle Opley fought to steady his horse.

"You're dead, Blake!" Matt cried.

Caulie huddled behind his horse's neck and aimed his pistol. Opley filled the sights, but when Caulie fired, a young cowboy moved into the line of fire. Caulie's bullet struck the drover in the cheek and toppled him from his horse.

"After him!" Matt screamed. The remaining cowboy waited for Opley to lead the way, though, and Caulie began his withdrawal. The dust stirred by the sudden charge of his companions had begun to settle, and Matt Simpson's aim improved as a result. The rifle barked twice in rapid succession. The first shot went wide, but the second struck Caulie's horse in the hindquarter.

Well, Caulie thought as he urged the stricken horse along, your luck finally let you down, Caulfield Blake. Opley, seeing the horse falter, charged. The Kansan fired as he rode, and Caulie shuddered as two bullets tore through the poor horse's ribs. As the animal went down, Caulie tried to jump clear, but it was too late. The horse landed on him, pinning both legs. Caulie glanced up as Opley bore down on him. The outlaw's face was agleam. Caulie raised his pistol and fired point-blank. The shot slammed through Opley's chest, and the killer slumped across his saddle as his horse raced past.

"Opley?" Matt called. "Doyle?"

Caulie fought to free his legs, but he knew there was no time. The horses were no more than seconds away. He reached out his left hand and touched the bloody flanks of his dead horse. He then smeared the side of his face with the sticky liquid. He eased his right hand under his hip so that the pistol was concealed.

"Well, looks like your grandpa's out three hundred dollars," the surviving cowboy declared as he gazed down at Caulie's still body.

"No, I'd say Grandpa just saved himself that bounty," Matt declared, passing Caulie by and riding along to where Opley's horse had come to a halt.

Caulie meanwhile felt his insides catch fire. He strained to hold his breath. The slightest motion spelled death.

"What you doing back there, Brad?" Matt called. "Haven't you seen enough? Come help me get Opley off this fool horse. He's carrying fifty, sixty dollars."

"Ain't you rich enough, Matt Simpson?" the cowboy asked, laughing.

"You know Grandpa. He keeps a tight rein on the cash box."

The cowboy rode along past, and Caulie gasped for breath. He inhaled a mixture of blood and sweat and dust and air. He held back a cough, then struggled to free his trapped legs. All the while he watched Matt and the cowboy. Both were occupied freeing Opley's feet from the stirrups. They'd managed to drop the outlaw's body to the dusty road when Caulie finally kicked free of his fallen horse. As they rifled through Opley's pockets, Caulie limped into the tangled wood alongside the road. He wormed his way between strands of barbed wire, then hobbled along. He paused atop a small hill and gazed down at the road as a half-dozen riders galloped up. Leading them was Henry Simpson himself.

"Matt, what's happened here?" the old man asked.

"We caught Blake himself down here on the road," Matt explained, hurriedly stuffing something that must have been Opley's money in a pocket. "Doyle got him, I suppose. He's dead."

"Dead? Who? I saw the boys back up the road. That Doyle Opley there with you?"

"And Caulfield Blake himself lyin' back there beneath his horse, Grandpa. You said you wanted him more than anybody. Put the run to Dix Stewart and a couple of boys, too."

"You mean to tell me there were four of 'em down here, and you lost three good men chasing 'em?" Simpson stormed. "Matt, you've got no sense at all, boy! You were to fire three shots the instant you saw anything!"

"Wasn't time, Grandpa. Blake just popped up from nowhere."

"More likely rode up the market road like he owned it," Simpson grumbled. "Four riders, and two of 'em boys. You let 'em shoot your company to pieces, kill the best gun hand on the range, then ride along by without so much as a howdy-do!"

"Grandpa, we shot Caulfield Blake!"

"Oh? And where'd you say you left him?"

"Right there 'neath his horse!"

"Well, this is past believing!" Simpson raged. "You sure it was Blake?"

"I saw him, too, Colonel," the cowboy standing beside Matt declared. "It was him, sure as the pastor preaches on Sunday."

"Then he's gone and slipped right through your fingers," Simpson said, spitting. "He's a snake, that one. I thought for sure my boys killed him the night he hung Austin, but with that one, you've got to make dead sure. He's up there somewhere right now, having himself a laugh at your expense."

"We'll find him," Matt pledged, gazing up the hill in Caulie's direction. "I swear it, Grandpa."

"You'll send more men up there to get killed?" the old man thundered. "Matt, you'll bleed us dry this way. We're no Yank army, and you're no General Grant to throw men away on a bet. No, son, there's a better way. He's afoot. He's going nowhere. For now."

"Later on he'll head for the Stewart cabin," one of the cowboys declared. "All we got to do, Colonel, is go on along in front of him."

Simpson smiled and waved his men on down the road.

"You up there, Blake?" the old man cried out at the surrounding hillside. "Are you? I'm doing myself some riding, Blake. We'll head on along, see how well a house can burn. And as to hangings, we might just see how well boys dance from oaks. Let you know how it feels to watch."

Caulie felt his insides die as he thought of the army on horseback that would charge Dix's cabin, that would sweep over the hill toward Hannah. He wanted to cry out, and if he'd had a rifle, he would have shot Henry Simpson stone-cold dead. But things being what they were, Caulie swallowed his rage and started toward the cabin. It was miles away, and a sense of urgency drove him along.

"Simpson, if you harm Hannah or my boys, I'll kill you," Caulie swore as he walked. "I'll kill you!"

Chapter Sixteen

It was better than four miles cross-country to Dix's cabin, and every inch of ravine and hillside seemed to hold some hidden peril with which to entrap Caulfield Blake. Briars and cactus thorns tore at his legs. Gopher holes trapped his ankles. And yet he struggled on as though life depended upon it. Indeed, Caulie suspected it did.

When he finally slipped through the barbed wire that marked the eastern boundary of the Diamond S Ranch and began limping the final mile and a half to the cabin, he felt oddly as if eyes were on his back. He never saw anyone, but the sandy soil was torn with hoofprints, and Caulie occasionally glimpsed a flash of steel or a bit of cloth on some surrounding hillside.

Lord, don't let me be too late, Caulie prayed. I've got to warn them.

He hoped young Carlos Salazar was on watch. The boy was still but half fit, but his eyes were those of a hawk. Roberto was steady as well. If only Simpson was cautious enough to allow Dix and the boys to settle in some before the attack. But that was almost more than one could hope for, and Caulie's darkest fear was that he'd stumble upon a scene of utter carnage. He recalled the town in northern Mississippi he and Dix had ridden through back in '64. Someone at a nearby farmhouse had shot a Yank captain from cover, and the bluecoat cavalry had taken its revenge. Animals were scattered everywhere, their hides so full of lead the meat could scarcely be eaten. Women and children cowered in the ruins of their houses. The men swung lifelessly from tree limbs.

They were riding hard, Caulie told himself. No one ever caught Dix Stewart on horseback. Zach and Charlie were quick as lightning. But they had the mules and the packhorse to goad along. It might prove a close thing.

As he crossed one hillside after another, Caulie kept an ear open for the sound of gunfire. He detected nothing more than an occasional stirring in the nearby thickets. Surely Simpson's riders were closing in, but each minute's delay offered Dix a better chance of defending the cabin.

Maybe Zach will head along home, Caulie thought. But more likely the boy would await his father's arrival. Or worse, Zach might race back in hope of locating Caulie along the road. Such a move spelled fast and certain death.

The nightmares reappeared. Caulie tried to blink them away, but pain and exhaustion were tearing at him like the teeth of pursuing hounds. When he finally climbed the ridge above Carpenter Creek and gazed out at the cabin, he was near finished.

Nothing appeared out of the ordinary. The mules grazed on the hillside. Their precious bundles of supplies had already been unloaded. Caulie searched the nearby corral for the packhorse or John Moffitt's pony. Neither was there. Maybe Zach had returned home after all.

Little Charlie was busy drawing water from the well. Rita was a few yards distant, hanging wash on a clothesline. Dix and the others were out of sight.

Wait just a bit longer, Simpson, Caulie thought as he struggled to make his way through the trees and on to the cabin. His legs were nigh numb now, and his blood-streaked face and torn clothes must have given him the haunting appearance of some specter come back to life. Still he felt the eyes on his back, the company of others. He drew out his pistol and reloaded the empty chambers. Any second he expected some horseman to pop out of the trees and deal him death.

It didn't happen. Instead, it was Caulie who emerged from the trees and slowly stumbled toward the cabin.

"Caulie?" Rita cried, dropping her clothespins as she hurried to greet him. "Whatever happened to you? Dix had us all giving you up for dead."

"There's time yet," he whispered. "Let's get along to the house."

"Are they out there?" she asked quietly.

"Probably got us in their sights this instant," he explained. "Go along. I'll fetch Charlie."

She turned, plucked her laundry basket off the ground, and started for the door. Caulie, meanwhile, stepped toward Charlie.

"Zach'll sure be relieved," the boy said as he cranked the windlass and drew the water bucket up from the well. "He went along home with the rest of the supplies. He'll likely come back later with a fresh horse."

"Better he stays," Caulie said as Charlie lifted the bucket up and set it on the stone wall of the well. "We've got company."

"Oh?" the boy asked nervously.

"Let's go," Caulie said, grabbing Charlie by the arm and starting for the door.

"My bucket!" Charlie objected, breaking loose from Caulie's weak grasp and rushing back to fetch the bucket. Caulie stared in disbelief as the air erupted. Shells slammed into the wall of the cabin, shattered windows and sent the livestock into a frenzy. Charlie barely touched the bucket when it exploded a hundred slivers of oak. Water splashed against the boy's face. He turned and dashed toward the house. Halfway there a blast from the woods tore through his side. Charlie fell like the last leaf of autumn, slowly, delicately, finally.

"No!" Caulie screamed, firing his pistol wildly as he limped toward the boy. Rifles protruded from the notches in the cabin wall, and the ambushers briefly held their fire. Caulie lifted Charlie in a single motion and started back toward the house. The sharp report of a rifle met Caulie's ears as a searing pain tore through his neck. He only just managed to hang on to Charlie while stumbling toward the door. It opened, and Dix helped both man and boy inside.

"Lord, help us," Dix said as he stared at his small, silent son.

"Dix, I . . ." Caulie started to say. He couldn't manage more, though. Already he could feel the warm flow of blood from his neck. A sharp pain cleared his eyes momentarily, then left his vision hazier than before.

"Rita, look after them," Dix said, returning to the wall. Only then did Caulie realize the cabin was nearly deserted. The Salazars had gone.

"I've got to . . ." Caulie objected as Rita examined his neck.

"Lie still a moment," she said, dipping a cloth in a pail of water that rested on the nearby table. "I believe they've taken a slice out of you."

"Charlie . . ."

"Yes," she said grimly. "In a moment."

Caulie closed his eyes a second and allowed her to treat the wound. Clearly he'd been lucky again. An inch to the right, and the bullet might have cut an artery. As it was, the pain and the bleeding would pass.

"There you are," Rita said as she tied the bandage in place. "You look like the devil, Caulie, but you're in little danger of dying."

"And Charlie?" Caulie asked as he opened his eyes. Rita was already busy examining the boy. A single bullet appeared to have torn through the boy's side.

"He's small, but I've seen him bounce back from a fever that would have carried anyone else off with it," Rita said, forcing a grin onto her face. "Go help Dix. That's what's needed. Lord knows I can patch up this child."

Caulie nodded, then blinked away his exhaustion. Dix pointed to an idle Winchester, and Caulie discarded his Colt. Outside, the shooting continued. Whenever Dix and Caulie paused, one of the encircling gunmen would attempt to close the distance. A tall cowboy with midnight-black hair made a move toward the well. Caulie shot him squarely in the chest. Another tried to rush the privy. Dix fired twice, and the intruder fell.

"Rush 'em!" a voice Caulie identified as Matt Simpson's yelled. The order went unheeded.

"Was one thing when Simpson had hired guns doin' his biddin'," Dix observed. "These ones are poor range cowboys, and they're way over their heads in deep water."

"I've known a range cowboy or two to shoot well enough to kill you," Caulie said. "Still, they don't seem too eager. What happened to the Salazars?"

"Rode over to Marsh's place while I went into town lookin' for you. Roberto thought it safer. Was right, it appears."

"You ever cover up that tunnel leadin' to the corral?" Caulie asked.

"No," Dix said, pausing to glance at the rug which covered a trapdoor concealing an escape tunnel dug years before in case of Indian attack. "What do you have in mind?"

"Where's the dynamite we packed out from town."

"Over by the fireplace," Dix answered. "Caulie?"

"What we need is a bit of artillery. This ought to do the trick."

Caulie pulled five explosive sticks from a flour sack, then took blasting caps and fuse. He added the dynamite to the sticks already in his pockets, then pulled aside the rug and stepped down into the tunnel.

"Caulie, you be careful," Rita urged.

"I'll try to be," Caulie said, brightening as he saw little Charlie's fingers move. "Let's see how Simpson likes this turn of events."

To call the moldy passageway beneath the cabin a tunnel was

to stretch the truth. It was scarcely wide enough to permit a grown man's shoulders to pass, and the years had caused the supporting planks to give way in places. Caulie worried the whole thing might have collapsed somewhere ahead. It was impossible to see anything, and as he crawled along, dragging his aching leg, he could only probe a few feet ahead with the butt of his rifle.

In the end, though, enough of the passage survived to allow him to crawl the twenty yards past the corral to the edge of the woods. The narrow opening at the other end needed widening, and Caulie was forced to claw away at the loose soil with his fingers. Finally he emerged on a slope just behind a large white oak. He blinked his eyes as the bright summer sun assaulted his vision. Then he began examining his surroundings.

The gunfire appeared to be concentrated about a hundred feet to his left, so he slowly circled in that direction. As he beheld a trio of cowboys firing steadily toward the cabin, Caulie attached the first fuse and cap, then lit the end. As it burned away the minutes, Caulie limbered up his right arm. When less than a minute remained of the fuse, Caulie tossed the dynamite. It twirled end over end through the air until it landed with a thud alongside the riflemen. They stared in disbelief, then scattered. Seconds later the air was split by the force of an explosion. Men flew in three directions.

Caulie lit a second fuse and continued. A pair of drovers rushed to rescue their companions. Caulie tossed his second stick so close to one that the cowboy nearly burned his foot on the flaming fuse.

"Good Lord!" the cowboy screamed, diving for safety. The dynamite blew a hole in the ground ten feet across.

Henry Simpson himself tried to rally his men. Those not too stunned by the dynamite to listen made a stand of sorts. Caulie tossed two more sticks toward the disorganized drovers, and they scattered like startled quail.

"Stop, men!" Simpson cried.

Caulie then threw a stack at Simpson, and the dynamite rolled to a stop less than five yards from the swaggering rancher.

Simpson dove to safety, but a companion was simply blown into pieces. The sight of their leader clawing the ground unnerved the others. They raced off in panic after their stampeding horses. Caulie thought to celebrate, but a rifle bullet which tore past his ear warned of other danger. Caulie sought cover.

"You must be a cat to have this many lives!" Matt Simpson called as he fired again. "I'll know better next time. I'll put a bullet right between those accursed eyes of yours."

"Won't be a next time, Matt," Caulie answered. "You're only good for shootin' small boys and jackrabbits. You're finished, you and that old man of a grandpa of yours. People are tired of you. Your day's over, Simpson!"

"No. It's you that's finished," Simpson yelled. "Matt, tend to him."

Matt's rifle opened up a steady, accurate fire, and Caulie limped off down the hill. He wove his way through trees and rocks until he could spot Matt's position. By that time it was too late. The Diamond S crew pulled out, leaving the silent summer afternoon to devour the lingering smoke.

Chapter Seventeen

Caulfield Blake knelt beside a pale Charlie Stewart and listened to the boy's labored breathing. It was hard to believe a thumbnail's worth of lead could tear at a body so. Rita had already dug the bullet from a rib, but even now blood seeped through the cotton bandages.

"He needs a doctor," Rita lamented.

"He can't be moved," Dix said, frowning heavily. "God, Caulie, that's my boy lyin' there! I can't just stand by and do nothin'."

"I know," Caulie said, nodding. "I'll ride out and collect the others. We'll be by for you around dusk."

"Don't be a fool. You're done in. Besides, they'll expect us," Dix warned.

"No, they'll be too busy talkin' and plannin' tomorrow. Only it's tonight they should concern themselves with 'cause there's not apt to be a tomorrow for some of 'em."

Dix nodded grimly. Caulie read his old friend's mind. It could prove to be the last night for others as well.

It wasn't a long ride to the Bar Double B. Caulie didn't bother saddling a horse. Instead he helped himself to a chestnut mare that wandered, bewildered, across the hillside.

"Your rider won't be missin' you, now will he, girl?" Caulie whispered as he climbed into the saddle. Soon he had the animal turned toward Carpenter Creek and the ranch that had once been home.

It wasn't an easy ride. Each time the horse jostled him, pain surged through him. Dix had been right. The day had taken its toll. Caulfield Blake was worn down to the bone. But he knew full well there'd never be as good a chance to find Simpson's crew off guard, to finish the whole business once and for all.

Carter was the first to see Caulie coming. The boy's face filled with concern, then relief. Caulie knew he was a sight, with face near black as coal from smoke and debris. Even the once white bandages around his neck were dark as night. He willed away the pain and nudged the chestnut mare onward. Carter rushed ahead to announce the arrival.

"Caulie, you look worse than when you came back from the war!" Hannah declared as she led Zach out to meet their weary visitor.

"There's been trouble," Marshall Merritt added. "Dix? Rita?"

"Still at the cabin," Caulie told them. "Charlie's been shot."

"Oh, no," Hannah cried. "Bad?"

"Bad enough. He's got pluck, that boy, but the bleedin' hasn't stopped," Caulie said, falling off his horse and stumbling into Zach's waiting arms.

"Come on, Pa," Zach said, leading Caulie toward the porch. "Ma, can he have somethin' to eat?"

Hannah flew past them toward the kitchen, mumbling to herself so that no one could understand. It was Marsh that spoke instead.

"You didn't come here to rest up, did you?" Marsh said solemnly. "You've come to get us to go with you . . . after those that did this to you."

"Yes," Caulie confessed. "The Salazars are here, too?"

"They've moved into the hay barn," Zach explained. "Once you're cleaned up, I'll fetch 'em."

"No time," Caulie objected. "I told Dix we'd meet him before dusk."

"There's time," Marsh said, easing an arm around Caulie's shoulder and helping him along. "An hour or two. You're in no shape to lead anybody anywhere just now. We'll need you for what lies ahead."

"Then you'll go?" Caulie asked.

"Don't see there's much choice," Marsh declared. "We're bound to be next. We hit them tonight, or else they come here in the morning."

Caulie nodded. Marsh and Zach helped him inside and deposited him on a sofa. Hannah soon appeared with some cold biscuits and slices of ham.

"I'm going, too," Zach declared as he worked to remove Caulie's boots.

"And me," Carter added from the kitchen door.

Caulie wanted to argue, but there was no point. Carlos Salazar would go, and Carter was no younger. In truth, the boys would be needed.

"You look in need of rest," Hannah said as she reappeared with a basin of hot water and a cloth.

"Later," he told her.

"Caulie, Marsh says you've got two hours left before you need to leave. Eat your food and rest."

He tried to grin at her angry face, but fatigue overwhelmed him. He managed to gobble the ham and biscuits. Then he lay back on the sofa and closed his eyes.

He barely felt Hannah's gentle hands washing his face. Likewise he didn't notice Zach exchanging his filthy, bloodstained shirt for a clean one. Instead Caulfield Blake drifted on a soft, wonderful cloud. The pain and the fatigue abated, and peace settled over him.

It didn't last. He was nudged awake by Zach as the evening shadows fell across the land. The sun was dying in the west. It was time to ride.

"I saddled the black," the boy explained. "Carter got your rifle all loaded. The Colt, too. Carlos brought Mr. Stewart over. We're all ready."

"I hate to drag you boys along to this," Caulie said, rubbing the sleep from his eyes. "I always thought the reason I was fightin' up in Tennessee was so you boys wouldn't have to."

"Ma always says life is a fight. You're always wrestling a drought or a flood, chills or fevers."

"Yes," Caulie said, recalling those words. Emma Siler had spoken them two decades earlier when he'd asked for Hannah's hand.

"I'll do like before, stay close to you, Pa."

"Good," Caulie said, touching the youngster's shoulder. Zach seemed suddenly younger, much too young for the purpose at hand.

"You ready yet?" Marsh called from outside.

"Shortly," Caulie said, buttoning his shirt and stepping into his boots.

Caulie made his way to the tall black stallion. The horse dipped his head in recognition, and Caulie warmed. It was good having a reliable mount beneath him.

"I followed their trail as far as the creek," Carlos said, pointing ahead. "They made for Siler's Hollow."

"So it appears," Dix agreed.

Caulie climbed into the saddle and gazed around him at the anxious faces of his companions. Carlos and Zach were intent, but Marsh and Roberto, though determined, were clearly fearful. Carter hung to the rear, his face ashen. Only Dix bore the face of a killer. His eyes were full of fire. Caulie knew that the memory of little Charlie's groans fed that fire.

"I've got words for you, men," Caulie announced, riding to the head of the meager column. "We're headed for battle, pure and simple. I want no reckless charges, friends. You boys stay behind Dix, Roberto, Marsh, and myself. When it's time to shoot, we'll let you know. If we're cautious and quiet, we ought to be able to slip in on 'em Comanche style, catch the whole batch off guard. But if it comes to shootin', then take your time, aim well, and shoot to kill. Because, my friends, they'll do just that, and I've buried too many friends on this land. Understand?"

"Yes, sir," the boys answered as one. Marsh nodded. Dix only stroked the cold stock of his rifle. Caulie waved them onward, then set the tall black stallion in motion.

A mile and a half down Carpenter Creek, Caulie picked up the trail. After another mile, the tracks of two horses broke off from the group.

"That's the Simpsons," Marsh observed, "the old man and Matt. They'll be up at the house. The others'd be down here."

"It's Simpson I want," Dix said angrily.

"Sure it is," Caulie said, pointing toward the house. "Only not tonight. Look close. That second horse is light. It carries no rider."

"Look here," Zach said, climbing down and pointing to the tracks leading to Siler's Hollow. "See the horse with the notched shoes?"

"That's Matt's horse," Carter added. "Johnny Moffitt told me about that. Matt had Ben Ames do it."

"A good way to mark your trail," Dix said, shaking his head. "Not too bright for a man who raids ranches."

"Could be that's the proof we'd need for a sheriff," Marsh argued. "Maybe we should . . ."

"Henry Simpson'd claim the horse was stolen," Caulie objected. "We all know what's to be done. If young Matt's down in the hollow, he could well be readyin' his crew for another raid. We go there."

The others muttered in agreement, and Caulie turned to follow the right-hand trail. As he wound along the creek, he motioned for the others to stay back a bit. He scouted ahead. Just below the shattered ruin of the dam a fire blazed brightly. Around it gathered several cowboys.

Caulie rode back and informed his companions. Then he led the way along a ridge, dismounted, and tied his horse to a nearby oak.

"Pa?" Zach whispered.

"Shhh," Caulie warned. "Follow me single column, and have your guns handy. Wait for the order to fire, though."

Caulie hobbled along the sandy trail toward the raiders' camp. It was barely fifty yards ahead, and the sounds of singing and laughter drifted past. Being downwind was an edge, and Caulie knew he needed every one he could find, what with so green a crew.

The faint light might have concealed Simpson's camp had not the fire been so substantial. Caulie counted seven blanket rolls surrounding the fire. Four men huddled together playing cards. The other three took turns drinking from a whiskey bottle.

Such arrogance, Caulie thought as he glared down at them. They sit out here in the open, just waiting for ambush. Have they so quickly forgotten what happened downstream? Well, they won't have a chance to learn from this mistake.

Caulie spread out his little company in a crescent. Dix and Carlos took one horn. Caulie and Zach took the other. Roberto, Carter, and Marsh occupied the center. Each crept closer until the camp was surrounded on three sides. The frothing waters of Carpenter Creek blocked escape to the north.

"If you ask me, Matt, we should've brought some dynamite ourselves," one of the cowboys argued between gulps of liquor. "That cabin'd be halfway to Austin by now."

"No, that would've been too easy," Matt said, laughing. "I thought how nice Katie Steward might be to the man who spared her folks. Then it turns out that runt brother of hers is all that's there with 'em. And Blake stumbles in right when we're ready to hit."

"He's not human!" a cowboy groused.

"Maybe not!" Caulie shouted. "Hold yourselves still, boys! You're covered."

"What?" Matt asked, rising to his feet. "Who's up there? Blake?"

"Expectin' me, were you?"

"Grandpa said you were a ghost, could creep up a man's spine and steal his hair like a blamed Comanche."

"So it'd seem."

"How many hands you got there with you? Can't be many? Or maybe you're all alone."

"Care to find out?"

"You'll need an army once Grandpa hears your shots."

"You won't care," Caulie said coldly. "You'll be dead."

"Ahhh!" Matt screamed, diving to the ground and grabbing a rifle. The others scrambled. Dix immediately opened fire from the right, and Caulie waved for the others to join in. In a matter of seconds three cowboys were torn apart by the rapid-firing Winchesters. A fourth made a break for the creek. Dix cut him down.

"All right!" Matt cried out. "We've had enough. Stop shooting!"

"We will," Dix answered. "Once you're dead!"

"Stop it!" Matt pleaded. "We're finished. Grandpa'll prove more than grateful when he hears you spared me. He might forget a lot of things. He'll never forgive you killing me, Blake. He never forgot what you did to Pa!"

Caulie felt a surge of anger rush through him. Dix was equally relentless. But Marsh Merritt called for a halt.

"He's right!" Marsh argued. "After all, he's little more than a boy himself."

"He's older'n Charlie!" Dix shouted. "Charlie never asked for any war! Neither did young Court Cabot!"

"And neither did I!" Matt cried, tossing his rifle aside and rising slowly. "It was all Grandpa's doing."

Caulie felt the power in his hands ebb. The boy standing

defenseless beside the fire wasn't the enemy. Henry Simpson was. Dix, for all his anger, could not shoot an unarmed seventeen-year-old.

"Drop your guns, you other two!" Marsh shouted.

The cowboys rose slowly and discarded their rifles. Caulie motioned for Marsh to wait, but perhaps the tall rancher didn't see. Carter followed as Marsh approached the camp. Caulie held Zach back, though.

"Pa?" Zach asked.

"Stay put," Caulie ordered as he crept closer. Marsh was but ten feet away when Matt held out an empty right hand in peace. At the same time young Simpson drew a pocket pistol with his left and fired.

"Oh, no," Marsh cried as the bullet blasted its way through his chest. Carter flung himself behind a rock as Matt fired a second time. The two startled cowboys gazed at their grinning companion in disbelief seconds before Dix and Carlos opened up with Winchesters. The first shots flung Matt Simpson back into the fire, his face and chest torn apart by bullets. A second volley struck down Matt's companions.

"Marsh!" Zach screamed, racing through the rocks toward the fallen figure of his stepfather. Carter was already kneeling over the dying rancher's bleeding body. Caulie turned away from them and limped to where Matt lay struggling to free himself from the flames.

"Why?" Caulie asked. "Why?"

Matt never answered. The young gunman's arm was near devoured by flame, and the lifeblood ran down his chest. His eyes fixed in a stare, and a shattered jaw dropped so that his mouth formed a ghastly silent grin.

"Caulie?" Dix asked moments later as he gripped his friend's arm.

"Why?" Caulie asked with blazing eyes.

"Who can say?" Dix mumbled as he dragged Caulie away to where Marsh's still body rested in the sand. "Can't train a dog all its life to bite anything that moves, then expect it to know gentle ways. Simpson twisted that kid, made him wild and unfeelin'. He couldn't wind up otherwise."

"I guess not," Caulie said, sighing as he gazed down at Marsh's shattered body. "I never should've given him a chance."

"It was Marsh's way," Zach said, reaching up and clasping Caulie's hand. "He believed in second chances. Lord knows he gave Carter and me enough of 'em. Ma, too. He knew she still had feeling for you, but it didn't keep him from coming around. Some held it against us, your helping hang Austin Simpson, but never Marsh."

"He was a good man," Caulie agreed.

"And now he's dead," Carter said, trembling.

"It's best we take him home," Roberto Salazar said, crossing himself as he knelt beside the body. "There is much to do."

"We're getting good at burying friends," Carlos added. "And fathers."

"I'll get the horses," Dix offered. "Give me a hand, Zach?"

"Sure, Mr. Stewart," Zach said, scampering up the hill.

"I'm sorry, Carter," Caulie said, grasping the boy's shoulders with weary hands.

"He wasn't much good at this sort of thing," Carter sobbed. "He should've stayed home."

"He chose to come."

"Felt he had to," Carter said, staring into Caulie's sad eyes. "Don't you see? You were going. He had to."

Yes, Caulie thought, nodding as Carter helped Roberto lift Marsh's corpse. Carlos brought over a horse, and the Salazars tied the body in place. Then Dix arrived with the other horses, and Caulie mounted the big black.

"I should see to Rita and Charlie," Dix said, excusing himself from the sad procession.

"I understand," Caulie said as his old friend departed.

Before the others could start up the trail, the sound of horses attracted Caulie's attention.

"Roberto, get the boys back home," Caulie called as he turned to meet the new menace. Roberto waved to the boys, but Zach and Carlos held their ground. Before Caulie could run the pair to safety, Henry Simpson and a trio of companions emerged from the trees.

"Hold up there, Simpson!" Caulie called. "Come another foot, and I'll shoot you."

"You!" Simpson cried out in surprise. "Matt?"

Caulie followed the old man's eyes until they fell on the corpse of his grandson. Henry Simpson turned pale, and the others drew back.

"Blake!" Simpson bellowed.

"There's been enough," Caulie cried. "We've each got dead to bury. It's time it was ended."

"It will be ended," Simpson swore. "Soon!"

Chapter Eighteen

Hannah sat on the hillside and waited anxiously for the return of Caulie, Marsh, and the boys. As the faint sounds of gunfire up the creek drifted across the land, a strange sense of foreboding descended on her.

"When is Pa coming back?" Sally asked as Hannah drew the girl onto one knee.

"Before long, Honeybee," Hannah said, stroking Sally's hair. "Wherever have your brothers gotten to?"

"They went to play with the Salazars," Sally explained.

Just as well, Hannah thought. She wished she could find some distraction herself. She finally lifted Sally to her feet, then stood and walked back to the house. Marsh always wanted dinner early, and he would likely be starving by the time he returned.

"Dear Marsh," Hannah thought as she stared out the window toward Carpenter Creek. He'd never been the gallant cavalier like Caulfield Blake. Marsh disliked violence, was grieved when a bobcat or a fox needed killing. Now he'd gone off to war.

The boys had gone, too. Of course, Carter was near as old as Caulie'd been the first time Comanches had raided the valley. But in some ways, Caulfield Blake had been born old, at least on the outside. There was a tenderness, a gentleness to him underneath, but it was scarcely ever gotten to by people. Carter was like that, too.

Zach she could read like the skies. His eyes reflected his feelings. Carter was cautious. Zach would leap into a thing with abandon. Maybe that was what worried her.

Marsh will have the good sense to use his head, Hannah told herself. And Caulie will never lead them into danger. No, they've got two fathers looking out after them. And the thought might have set her at ease had anyone other than Henry Simpson stood against them.

She had potatoes cut and on the boil and greens bubbling away beside them when she heard horses splash through Carpenter Creek. Instantly she took a shotgun from the gun closet and loaded both barrels. She then stepped outside and awaited the riders.

The moment she saw Carter's hollow cheeks, Hannah knew there'd been death. A bundle slumped across one of the horses. In the darkness she could barely make out the faces of the riders, and her heart ached.

"Zach?" she cried out. "Caulie?"

"No, not him," Carter said as he slowly rolled out of his saddle.

Hannah gazed sadly at Roberto Salazar, then stepped closer to the horsemen. Carter blocked the path.

"Ma, he was right beside me," Carter explained. "The shooting was supposed to be over."

"Oh, no," she cried as she spotted Marsh's checkered shirt.

"Was Matt Simpson, Ma. He hid a pocket Colt. It was all over."

"Oh, Marsh," she sobbed, dropping to her knees. "Zach? Caulie?"

"They're coming," Carter assured her. "Ma, he didn't suffer. It happened so quick I don't think he even knew it."

"Oh, no," she cried, weeping openly. "Not Marsh."

Chapter Nineteen

She was still crying when Caulfield Blake appeared. Zach climbed down and raced over to his mother. Caulie remained at a distance.

"Hannah, I'm so sorry," he told her. "I don't know quite what happened."

"I told her," Carter said, turning angrily toward Caulie. "He'd never gone if not for you."

"Hush, Carter," Hannah barked. "He went because of us. We were in danger, and he felt he had to protect us."

"But if *he* hadn't come back . . ." Carter argued.

"We might all be dead," Hannah said bitterly. "It's not your father you should call to account, Carter. It's Henry Simpson."

"*My* father's up there on that horse," Carter said, swallowing a tear. "As for Simpson, he's got his own sorrow. Matt's dead."

Hannah's face grew paler, and she rose to her feet.

"Caulie, he'll come for us now," she said, fighting to control her trembling hands.

"I know," he said. "But we've got other business to attend first."

Caulie, weary as he was, climbed down from his horse and limped to the toolshed. He grabbed a spade and started for the small fenced enclosure where Blakes had always laid their dead to rest.

Zach appeared shortly carrying a pitch torch. He set the torch firmly in place, then reached for the spade.

"See to the horses, son," Caulie said, resting a heavy hand on the boy's back. "Then see to your ma. She'll need a shoulder to lean on for a time."

"You've got one, too," Zach reminded him.

"Wouldn't be proper . . . or right. Leave me to do what I know all too well. I've dug here before."

"Yes, sir," Zach said, leaving reluctantly.

Yes, Caulie thought as he watched the dark-haired boy cross the tree-studded ground toward the house. I've buried the best of me here. There, to his right, lay the twin graves of his parents. On the left stood the simple marker etched with Caulie's brother Lamar's name. Lamar lay back in the Tennessee hills somewhere, felled by Yank muskets leading the charge. It seemed a cold, lonely place to die, and so Caulie had set up a stone for his brother on the dear, precious hill overlooking Carpenter Creek.

"Seventeen," Caulie mumbled as he dug into the sandy soil. "Hardly old enough to die." Matt Simpson had been seventeen, too. Often life was short. How sad to spend so much of it hating and killing and destroying!

Caulie finished the grave, then pulled the torch out of the ground and hobbled back to the house. The darkness swallowed the graveyard, and except for the torch, the whole world appeared to vanish in the night. Off in the distance lightning split the heavens.

163

It should storm tonight, Caulie thought as he extinguished the torch in the sandy ground outside the house. It's been a violent day. Why should nightfall change things?

Following a near-silent supper, Caulie slipped outside. He spread a pair of blankets across the porch and reloaded his Winchester.

"Pa?" Zach asked from the doorway. "I've got my bed ready for you."

"It's best I pass the night out here," Caulie explained.

"Why?"

Caulie frowned. How could he explain it? He didn't belong in that house, not tonight. In death the place belonged to Marshall Merritt as it never had in life. And Caulie was, more than ever, an outsider.

"Pa?" Zach asked again. "It looks to be a storm brewing. Come along inside."

"Not tonight," Caulie told the boy. "It's best I keep watch. And folks would think ill of my movin' in with Marsh lyin' dead in there."

"Folks? You mean Carter."

"He's a right to feel pain, Zach."

"We all do," Zach said, stepping outside and helping Caulie out of his boots. "I could split the watch with you."

"No, your brothers and sister will need you near."

Zach nodded and returned to the house. It saddened Caulie to feel the awful silence descend on him. But it was bound to be.

Caulie slept uneasily. The storm came, but pelting rain and harsh winds were nothing to the uneasiness brought on by the knowledge that Henry Simpson was out there in the distance, even now plotting revenge. Twice Caulie awoke at the crackling of twigs on the ground beside the house. The first time Caulie spied a skunk. The other instance a raccoon prowled the night. In the end, though, Simpson was occupied elsewhere.

"I hope that lasts," Caulie whispered as he watched the sun

break the eastern horizon. But even as he spoke the words, he knew it was not to be.

An hour after daybreak Caulie collected the family and led the way to the graveyard. Carter and Zach escorted their mother, sister, and brothers. The little boys stared at the hole with wide, unknowing eyes. Roberto and Carlos Salazar carried the body, now wrapped in a favorite quilt. The rest of the Salazar clan followed, whispering prayers in Spanish and making the sign of the cross.

"Caulie, won't you read something?" Hannah asked, passing a Bible into his dirt-stained hands.

"I'm not so much for readin' another's words," Caulie said, turning the book over in his hands. "My ma found comfort in this book, but I've rarely found much consolation in the death of a friend, of a good man like Marsh Merritt."

Carter gazed up in surprise, and Caulie continued.

"I'd like to leave a preacher to read verses over this grave," Caulie said, taking a deep breath. "What I've got to say comes from my heart. Just now we're all burdened with sadness. Marsh Merritt proved himself a good man, steady as a rock when the moment called for it. He did right by his family, loved 'em deeply, and gave his life that they might be safe. He's left behind a fine legacy in the memories of his wife, Hannah, his daughter, Sally, and the four boys."

"Amen," Carter said, gripping his mother's hand.

"I know each of you will have some private thoughts to pass along, so as we set our brother Marsh in this hallowed ground, I leave you to say your own good-byes."

Caulie helped the Salazars place Marsh's body in the soggy grave. He then stepped aside as each of the others filed past and sprinkled dirt over the corpse.

"Good-bye, Pa," Carter said, kneeling beside the trench.

Zach whispered something, then led Sally along. Hannah came last of all. She held the twins tightly. The bewildered boys kept glancing around in search of Marsh. It tore at Caulie's heart to read the confusion in those tear-filled eyes.

Carlos stayed to help fill in the grave. Caulie shoveled a few inches of dirt into the hole, then passed the spade and tried to rub the soreness out of his back.

"They will come soon," Carlos said as he scooped dirt into the open grave. "I saw his eyes."

"Yes," Caulie agreed. "Won't be long now."

"I know this Simpson. He will bring them all this time."

"Likely," Caulie agreed. "And then it will be over."

They filled in the grave completely, then tamped down the dirt. A stone would be placed later. Caulie hoped there would be need of but one.

Caulie passed the morning nervously watching the slope leading to Carpenter Creek. Except for accepting a platter of ham and eggs from Zach, Caulie spoke to no one. Finally there was a movement from across the creek, but it wasn't Henry Simpson.

Dix Stewart drove a wagon into the shallows of the creek, then continued across the stream and along toward the house. Caulie limped out to greet his old friend. As the wagon drew closer, Caulie saw that Rita sat in the bed with little Charlie's head resting on her knee.

"What's wrong?" Caulie called to them.

"Riders!" Dix shouted, pointing behind him. "Three or four round sunrise. Others followin' along. I figured we'd have a better chance together."

Caulie nodded as he pulled himself up on the seat beside Dix. Gazing back toward the creek, Caulie detected a pair of horsemen. Simpson! But at least the old man hadn't sent an army at them, as he might have.

Dix drove the wagon as far as the house before pausing. Caulie climbed down and hobbled around back. He took a barely conscious Charlie in his arms and carried the boy to the porch.

Zach swung the door open wide, and Caulie continued on inside. Hannah conducted him back to the boys' room and pointed to Zach's bed. Caulie laid Charlie on the bed, and Hannah spread a blanket over the injured boy.

"I was so sorry to hear about Marsh," Rita said, clutching Hannah's hands. "It seems to be a summer of death."

"Yes," Hannah said, frowning as she brushed back a strand of dirty blond hair from Charlie's forehead. "It's a hard life out here sometimes. Poor Charlie. He isn't feverish?"

"That's passed. The bleeding's better as well."

"Given time, boys have a way of mending," Hannah said, swallowing her own sadness.

"He'll have that time," Caulie said, running his fingers along Charlie's shoulder. The boy's eyes cracked open, and a faint smile came to his lips. Caulie supplied a grin of his own, then turned to join Dix outside.

Zach and Carter were already there. Each of the youngsters cradled a long-barreled Winchester. Caulie followed their eyes to the creek where a half-dozen riders were forming up. At their head rode Henry Simpson. The old man shouted orders and waved his hands wildly. The cowboys glanced around as if bewildered.

"They don't seem any too eager to approach," Dix noted. "Not too many of 'em, either."

"No," Caulie agreed. "Could be they've turned cautious."

Well, we've killed a few of 'em, Caulie thought as he grimly watched the approach of the Diamond S riders. These were no gunmen with Simpson this time, just range cowboys. It was hard to find hatred for such men. Henry Simpson, though, was a different matter.

"Zach, best run down to the barn and bring the Salazars to the house," Caulie suggested. "Not much cover back that way. Get that wagon out of the way, too."

"Sure, Pa," Zach said, scampering away.

"Carter, you take the front window," Caulie instructed. "But first make sure the little ones are out of the way."

Carter nodded and set about the task.

"So, it's come down to this," Dix grumbled as he readied himself for the upcoming melee. "Seems as if we've done this before."

"Once or twice."

"Seems strange that so many should've died for one man's greed."

Caulie nodded, then grimly waited for Zach to return with the Salazars. Simpson had finally persuaded his cowboys to cross the creek. The riders now closed the distance slowly, cautiously.

"Zach, they're comin'!" Caulie shouted.

The boy soon appeared, leading the Salazar family along toward the back door. Caulie motioned Dix toward the house, then followed his old friend inside.

Simpson led his company up the hill not so much intentionally as from the fact that the others seemed reluctant to ride ahead of their boss. Simpson himself was furious. Even as he neared the house, he waved violently toward his crew.

"I said to ride!" the old man screamed. "There aren't but a few of them left. They killed my son. Now they've killed Matt, too!"

Simpson himself made no move, though, and the others held back. Caulie stepped to the door as Zach conducted Roberto and Carlos Salazar down the hall to the front room.

"Watch the side windows," Dix instructed. "Be ready."

"They're in range already," Carter pointed out. "Shouldn't we open up?"

"Be patient," Caulie said as he stepped out onto the veranda. "Simpson, hold it right there!"

"I've come for you, Blake!" Simpson responded.

"You?" Caulie said, laughing. "You old fool, you're licked. You've not got any Olie Swain or Doyle Opley with you now. These are workin' cowboys. They didn't ride up here to get killed!"

"They do as I say!" Simpson said, again gesturing to his companions. One or two started, but Dix fired a shot in front of the first, and Carter fired just short of the second.

"Go home, boys!" Caulie called. "There's been enough killin'."

"We mean you no harm, Mr. Blake!" the nearest drover called.

"Coward!" Simpson yelled, pulling a pistol and firing at the cowboy. The young rider stared in disbelief as a bullet tore into his shoulder.

"Colonel?" the wounded cowboy called.

"Now the rest of you get after them!" Simpson yelled. "Go on!"

"Can't you see it's over, Colonel Simpson?" a drover with bright red hair asked.

Simpson turned to fire again, but the wounded cowboy pulled a pistol and fired first. Henry Simpson rocked in his saddle, then stared wild-eyed at Caulie before falling earthward.

"Like I said, it's over!" the redheaded cowboy called down to Caulie. "We're headed home. We leave you to your range."

The cowboys gathered around their wounded comrade and assisted him along. In what seemed an impossibly brief time, the cowboys recrossed Carpenter Creek and vanished into the obscure horizon. Caulie, meanwhile, made his way slowly to where Henry Simpson's body lay in a pool of blood.

"Well, old man?" Caulie called. "Have you brought enough death to this land at last?"

The old rancher's eyes stared blankly at the sky, but Caulie found no sympathy for his old nemesis. There had been too much pain, too many lost years and interrupted dreams.

"Leave him!" Dix called. "Leave him for the hawks!"

"No, it's best he's buried in town. We'll load him in the wagon."

"We'll take him in," Roberto Salazar spoke up from the porch. "If we can borrow your wagon, Senor Stewart."

"Take it," Dix said, shaking his head. "Come on, Caulie. Let's go see Charlie."

Chapter Twenty

Caulie sat on one of the small beds in the corner of the boys' bedroom while Dix Stewart visited with his son. Charlie was still pale as death, but a sparkle of life had returned to his eyes, and somehow Caulie knew the boy would recover. Hannah had said it. The young always seem to mend.

Caulie knew other wounds would heal as well. The small ones who slept in the two miniature beds would recover in time from the death of their father. Even now little Todd and Wylie began to realize Marsh would not reappear. There were no tears, just a sort of bewildered whimpering that pained Caulie all the more because he could do so little to soothe it.

It will pass, Caulie assured himself. They've got brothers around that can teach them to ride, to rope steers and make river crossings. They've got a strong mother who can put steel in their backbones.

In a way, Caulie even envied them. At least they belonged somewhere. Caulfield Blake already felt himself drifting again.

"Where will you go now?" Dix asked a half hour later as the two of them prowled the hillside. "Back to the Clear Fork?"

"I've got horses there," Caulie explained.

"Hannah will need somebody now."

"She's got Zach and Carter. They're not boys anymore to have their hands held crossin' streams or their tails blistered for prankin' neighbors. They're men."

"They'll have needs, too," Dix argued. "Stay. I can read her eyes, Caulie. You'd be welcome."

"Maybe in time."

"Now! If you don't feel right livin' under her roof, take the cabin awhile. Or come to town with us. Lord knows there's work enough for a dozen Caulfield Blakes there, what with the store a shambles."

"You might give thought to hirin' the Salazars, Dix."

"No, they've vowed to return to Ox Hollow. Folks want their own fields to tend, you know."

"I'd like to stay," Caulie admitted. "I want to. I need them. But it's not for me to say."

"Do this for me, Caulie. Don't let that mule stubbornness send you runnin' away again. Your place is here, on this very land where your folks lie buried."

"They're not the only ones buried here now," Caulie said, turning away. And the shadow from Marsh's grave fell clearly across Hannah's door.

Dix and Rita prepared to return to town a little after midday. Caulie helped pack Charlie in the bed of a Bar Double B wagon.

"You'll come visit?" the boy asked, brightening some as Caulie gripped his small, terribly cold fingers.

"Be chasin' you down the creek in a week," Caulie promised.

"I'll hold you to that," Dix declared as he helped Rita into the bed. "The both of you."

171

The wagon then headed off south toward the junction of the market road, and Caulie felt terrifyingly alone. Zach then took his hand and led the way toward the barn.

"Thought we might give the horses a good brushing," Zach said. "If you're up to it."

"I am."

"Seems like just yesterday you were riding in," Zach mumbled. "Things have gotten awful quiet. The Salazars have gone, and now the Stewarts leave. Todd and Wylie won't go down to the creek without Carter or me along. Sally just sits with Ma and holds the knitting yarn. It's like . . ."

"Someone died?" Caulie asked. "Someone has."

"When Grandma Siler died, we all had a good cry and then got on with things. This time is different."

"It's expected somehow for old people to go. She was sick awhile, too."

"Marsh wasn't. One minute he was walking tall and proud. The next he was dead."

"Bullets do a fair job of cuttin' a man down."

"Pa, Carter says you'll likely leave. You won't, will you?"

"It'd seem best. My work's finished."

"Finished? You just got here." Zach walked away a minute, then returned and leaned against his father's weary side. "I know you've got business up north, but it can wait a bit, can't it? We'll ride up there and help you later. We need you."

"Simpson's dead."

"You think a father's just for blowing up dams and killing the likes of Henry Simpson? No. We need you now more'n ever. Ma especially."

"People will talk."

"They talked before. We never paid 'em much mind."

"I won't have folks think ill of your ma."

"Just let 'em try. Besides, a ranch needs a man's hand. Ma told me that herself."

"You and Carter are old enough."

"And what about us? We need you, too."

172